The Billionaire's Song

The Complete Series

A BWWM BILLIONAIRE ROMANCE

Jaelynn McCranie

Publisher's Note: This is a work of fiction. Names,
characters, places, and incidents are a product of
the author's imagination. Locales and public
names are sometimes used for atmospheric
purposes. Any resemblance to actual people, living
or dead, or to businesses, companies, events,
institutions, or locales is completely coincidental.

The Billionaire's Song/ Jaelynn McCranie -- 1st ed.
Xplicit Press, an imprint of TLM Media LLC

ISBN-13: 978-1-62327-659-1
ISBN-10: 1-62327-659-4
eISBN: 978-1-62327-660-7

Printed in the United States of America

CONTENTS

1

Malibu sunsets are really the most beautiful. The colors of everything in heaven and on earth seem to dance in the sky, making it seem that they are all fighting for the attention of the observer. Trenton Lively likes nothing more than to watch these sunsets over the top of his champagne glass, totally ignoring the bustle about him, everyone getting ready for yet another party at his sprawling estate. Trenton is tired of these parties, but he understands their value, for his business, and actually for his life.

At 38, Trenton has really come into great fortunes. Granted it was by the way of great tragedy, but he really had no way of foreseeing or preventing, the accident in the south of France thirteen years earlier, the accident that took both his parents and his sister. Trenton really had no desire at the time to travel with his family, intent to party instead at every opportunity, something which has not changed in over a decade.

The music business is hard, but Trenton has no idea of how hard. His parents managed to staff their record label with very competent people, the kind of people who really want to see the label succeed, and who are invested, seriously invested in the longevity of the business. It is very rare, and hard indeed to find staff so devoted, so committed to the success of a business in which they have no vested interest. But that is certainly the case with Live Records.

As the sun sets, preparations are completed for the party, and the guests start to trickle in. Trenton wears a t-shirt and jeans, much unlike the effort that the other guests have put in, but he really doesn't care. Already three bottles of champagne in his system, the gathering starts to feel a little more pleasant. Already he begins to throw his eyes around, looking for the first willing mouth to wet his cock. There are benefits to these soirees, and all of them, at least for him, are of the sexual kind. It is amazing what women are willing to do for just the promise of a recording deal, and Trenton really is in the perfect position to make these promises.

He makes his way through the various rooms that house the party, most of the bottom floor of his house and onto the terrace, greeting everyone pleasantly enough, keeping everyone feeling comfortable enough in his presence. There is an unspoken resentment that permeates the room, though, an extreme dislike of his entitlement, and how he seemed to have just stumbled into his fortune, not actually working a day in his life for it. Trenton doesn't really care, though, knowing that in some way everyone here tonight is dependent on him for their own success.

A band takes to the stage set up on the terrace and immediately belts out a rock ballad that fills the space in its entirety. The raspy sound of the lead vocalist fills the space and seems to almost envelop the house. For a moment, everyone seems to turn towards the stage and give them a minute of their attention before they return to the nothing that they were doing. To call what they were doing nothing is an understatement, though, because everyone seems to be intent on spotting one or two pieces of ass to bed later, or shortly, whichever comes first.

The band quickly becomes background, and Trenton continues his movements through the crowd, being pleasant enough with everyone that he meets, actually making quick work of every glass in his hand. The glasses change quickly too, and although you wouldn't guess it looking at him, he is already quite drunk. His eyes start to take on the look of lust too, and Trenton throws them across the various groups of people, singling out the women in the groups. Who will wet his cock tonight, he wonders?

He sees a group of girls, no older than 20, and he makes his way to them. They are obviously working girls, and he doesn't mind. These parties need a few of this type around, just to make sure that everyone is at least sexually satisfied after this soiree. Sex is really a powerful tool to use in these situations, and so sex hangs in the background just waiting to be pounced upon. Everyone is willing to take and be taken, and this probably has more than a little to do with the free-flowing cocaine too.

A tray makes its way past Trenton, and he turns towards it. The waitress lifting it up to him is dressed in nothing but a bikini, and he looks at her breasts for a moment and then works his eyes down her belly. She doesn't seem interested in him, though and just lifts the tray up so that his view is suddenly blocked. He brings his nose down on the straw and sniffs in three lines into each nostril before the waitress moves on. He watches her walk away, his eyes firmly on her ass before he remembers the most promising prospects that are immediately to his right.

One of the women, who introduces herself only as Cee-Cee, comes in closer and runs her finger across the outline of Trenton's cock, almost immediately. His dick is thick and long, but it is not hard, yet. He has a few things going on in his mind, and so he throws his eyes around the space again, probably looking for another girl or two to add to the party, but then taking his hand in hers and pressing her fingers against his cock. She moves her fingers on his meat firmer now, up and down, and his cock pulses a couple of times, still not hardening, though.

The woman looks like she won't take no for an answer, and Trenton starts to think about what it is that she might want from him. Everybody seems to want something from him. He looks at her mouth, her full lips with the slightest hint of nude lipstick, stark against the paleness of her face. Her hair is just the right combination of black and fiery red to make it attractive, and he wishes to himself that it was tied back. Trenton has a thing for women who don't feel the need to hide their faces with hair.

With her hand still on his cock, he pulls her away from the group that she was standing with. They walk passed the other clusters of people, Trenton stopping momentarily to address a few people, not really interested in what they are saying to him, thoughts already going to Cee-Cee's mouth on his cock, which is hardening slightly at her grip at last. He looks around the bottom floor of his house as they come off the terrace, thinking of the nearest appropriate place for his encounter with this semi-redhead.

He thinks that the study will suit him just fine, and so he pulls her towards the open door. There cannot be anybody inside he thinks, nobody at the party drunk enough to fuck with the door open. Trenton throws his eyes around the room as soon as he enters it, and then closes the door with Cee-Cee, locking it behind her back. She is already going down to her knees, already working on his zip, already freeing his cock from his jeans. She slips his soft head into her mouth and sucks on it. His cock isn't hard enough yet though, so she starts to stuff the softness into her mouth.

Trenton undoes his button, and his jeans fall to just below his butt. The woman sucking on his soft meat pulls them further down until they are around his knees. Then she starts to feather his balls, impressed at their sheer size. Trenton has always been proud of his cock. But he has been more proud of his massive balls. She pulls on them now, gently, as his cock starts to take real shape in her mouth now. She almost sighs a huge sigh of relief, not realizing that it's the cocaine playing tricks on Trenton's dick, as it does.

His erection seems to be playing along now, though, and he shuffles back into the room, taking Cee with him. She follows, on her knees, until they get to the large leatherback behind the desk. Trenton falls into the chair, and Cee immediately is on his penis again. She starts to work her mouth up and down the first few inches of the thickness. It really is an incredibly thick cock, and she really struggles to get way down the huge shaft. But she tries, all the same, really wanting to please him.

And please him she does. His cock is suddenly a solid scepter, rock hard and as long as it is going to get. It must be thirteen or fourteen inches, she thinks, managing to get halfway down the tool now. This is as far as she is going to be able to go, so she knows that she has to get creative if she is going to have any hope of pulling an eruption from the cock that is piercing her throat now. She sucks on this half for a moment longer, trying to read from the sounds coming from Trenton whether he is enjoying it or not. He doesn't make a sound, though.

She pulls her mouth off over his head and gives it a few licks. Then she works her tongue around the base of his cock and gives it a long lick up until the head again. Again she goes down to the base and licks it all the way up. Over and over she licks it, like an ice-lolly, settling on the head for the briefest of moments every time she gets to the tip again. Still, not a sound can be heard from Trenton, and Cee gets more than a little frustrated.

When she gets up to his head again, she sucks on it harder than before. Then she starts to nibble on it, finally drawing soft moans from the man that she really is intent on pleasing. She has always thought of herself as a master cock sucker, but Trenton is really working on her ego, fighting it at every turn. She nibbles a little harder, and then bites into the head, carefully, though. Trenton moans a little louder, but he doesn't tell her to stop, letting her know that she is starting to get the hang of his dick, starting to do what he really likes.

She returns to sucking on half of the dick again, just to spice things up a bit. Again Trenton is silent, but his erection is going nowhere, so she knows that even though he is not responding to her, he is enjoying it. Then she bites the head again, but only briefly, before sinking her teeth down the shaft on the descent. She bites into it on the way up to, until she is again biting into his head. A little harder, a little deeper with her teeth, and Trenton's moans become soft groans. She seems to really be doing something right now.

Then she licks it again, from the base all the way to the head, working her tongue in slow circles around the dome, and the licking her way back down. She alternates between licking, sucking and biting now, her biting having more of an audible effect than any other action, though. She doesn't mind because still he is rock hard, solid and starting to ooze precum. Then she thinks of another idea, one that she is sure he will appreciate, just because his balls are so fucking huge.

She pulls her mouth off his cock completely and settles her nose in his nut sack. She sniffs in the scent of his balls, enjoying it immensely, moving her nose from side to side across the surface of his balls. Then she takes one of them in her mouth, between her teeth, pulling on the flesh just before sinking her teeth into the orb. As he starts to moan, she releases it, moving across to the other one, doing exactly the same thing to this orb too. Cee-Cee moves this way from ball to massive ball, the moments that she bites into them longer each time.

After a while, she tries to take both of them in her tiny mouth, but it is just not possible. She tries to put them on top of each other, tries to manipulate them this way and that, but they are just too damn big. She gives up the fight and returns to her one at a time strategy. It works well enough, at least for her, and she bites a little harder into the one in her mouth. He lets out a yelp, and she knows that perhaps she has gone too deep this time.

"Yes, yes, that's it... bite my fucking balls bitch..." he says, though, and so she does. She really always thought that the balls were the most sensitive part of a man, but clearly not with Trenton. She bites harder still, and he yelps louder and louder. She runs her fingers up and down his shaft as she really gets stuck into his nuts with her teeth now. She almost thinks that he is going to just spray her hands and hair with cum at any moment now because he is making constant moans now. But then again he is silent, and she is sucking the tip of his dick again.

Trenton must feel that she deserves a reward for her efforts, or he could just be bored with her trying to pull an orgasm from him, and he suddenly stands up. He pulls her to her feet and lifts her onto the table. He lifts her skirt high above her waist and is not surprised at all that she isn't wearing any panties. He touches her clit with the tip of his finger and finds it absolutely soaked. She really enjoyed sucking his cock, he thinks.

He pushes hard against her clit with

the tip of his finger and then presses harder still. He starts to move his finger around in circles, pressing them deeper into her, against her pussy. Then he works his other finger between her cunt lips and teases her hole. He runs the finger along the slit, parting her lips more and more but not going into her at all. She moans loudly, though, half in anticipation of what he is threatening to do, half because of what he is doing to her clit.

The finger running lines up and down her slit suddenly presses against her hole and makes its way all the way inside her. There is no resistance too, mostly because her pussy is so absolutely wet. He fingers her briefly with this finger, the other still pushing hard against her clit, and then he pulls out and away from her. He runs the finger that was just inside her along her lips and then forces it into her mouth. She sucks on it with as much skill as she just showed on his cock. He looks at her eyes, checking for her responses to the taste of herself.

Trenton returns the smile that he gets from Cee now, and as he adds a second finger into her along with the one that he just removed from her, her smile becomes a soulful moan, and he likes it. He adds a third finger just because, and to counter the wetness that he finds there, and it works. Suddenly the fit is tight, and Trenton likes the feeling of her pussy now. He digs really deep into her now, and pulls a mild orgasm from her, much to his obvious delight.

He pulls his fingers from her and feeds them into her mouth again. Her eyes close, and she sucks on his fingers hard. She really seems to enjoy the taste of herself, and Trenton really likes the fact. He looks down at his own cock now and notices that he is losing his erection. He doesn't need to be hard to cum, though, he knows this from previous experience, but it is nice. It is always nicer to be hard just before you blow your load, but he starts to think that there might not be time for him to get hard before he shoots, remembering that there is a whole party going on outside that needs his attention.

Trenton pulls her off the table again, and he stands against the side of it, pushing her down on his now soft cock. He pushes it against her lips and then into her mouth. She takes it inside her mouth almost completely, sucking on the thick softness very hard. Her aim is to get him hard again, but it doesn't seem like it is going to happen. But when she starts chewing on the soft meat, it pulses a little, and then a lot. Then it gets harder and harder, and with a semi-hard on, he starts to fuck her mouth rather wildly.

There is no time for him to think about the state of his cock now, all he knows is that he needs to, really wants to, have an orgasm. There will be plenty of other mouths on his cock before the night is over, and maybe a few pussies too, so there really is no rush for the epic blow that he so desperately wants. He just needs to empty his cock now and get back to the party for a little while. His cock is about two thirds hard now, though, so he knows that his climax won't be disappointing.

"Pull on my balls... pull my fucking balls hard..." he instructs her. She obeys him and starts to squeeze and pull on his nuts with his cock still in her mouth. He starts to moan louder, and then a little louder. He keeps on thrusting into her mouth, really hitting the back of her throat now. She pulls harder still, trying to ignore the cock that is so deep in her mouth now that she cannot breathe. She doesn't care, though because she senses that she has him on a collision course with his orgasm now.

His cock doesn't get any harder, though, in fact getting a little softer. He is a little frustrated, so he fucks her mouth a little harder. His focus is on the fingers that are really tugging on his balls now, squeezing them harder and harder, pulling the sack and balls further away from his groin. He starts to yelp a little, then a lot, and he goes deeper into her mouth. Finally, he sees the pending orgasm approaching.

Harder and harder he pushes his cock into her mouth and brings himself closer to climax. He forgets about her completely now, all thoughts on the fingers pulling incredibly hard on his sack now, and on the hot mouth on his dick. His head starts to pulse some more, and then a whole lot more. He knows that he is going to blow at any moment now, and so he looks down at her, wanting to see her response to his load in her mouth. Surely she is going to swallow because there is nowhere else for her to rid herself of the semen that at any moment is going to make an appearance.

When he starts to cum, he is caught almost by surprise. He looks away from her for a moment and then looks back down at her. She doesn't skip a beat and just swallows his load as it escapes his cock. Trenton is a little impressed. Actually, he is more than a little impressed, and as he watches her swallow every drop of his seed and then nibble on his dick head before sucking on it, making sure to get the last drops of semen from the tip, he taps her face lightly on the side. Then he pulls his cock from her mouth slowly.

She licks his balls for a moment and then bites into them a little bit. Then she gets up and pulls herself together, watching Trenton stuff his cock back in his pants. She isn't sure if he wants to kiss her, not sure because he is looking at her neck, and then at her mouth. Then he sends a hand under her skirt and pulls her panties to the side, settling his finger inside her. He starts to finger her with just half of his finger and doesn't move his eyes from hers.

After bringing her to another orgasm, his way of saying thank you, he pulls the finger from her and puts it in his own mouth. He sucks on it, really sucks on it, and then places the finger in her mouth. She sucks her thank you off the finger and then adjusts her underwear and her skirt. Trenton looks around for the bar and then finding it he opens a bottle of champagne. The room has been recently renovated, so he is glad that he found the alcohol rather easily.

They swig back a couple of glasses, having a conversation about nothing at all really, but it is not uncomfortable. Then they leave the room and lose each other on the terrace, not really saying goodbye to each other, not really needing to. Trenton is pulled away by some executives who have something to say about the talent here tonight, but he isn't really interested in. He has always found a way of passing the buck onto his executives, something that they don't mind, but they need to make an effort to keep him involved in the business. After all, it is his family business, and Trenton is the king of this particular castle.

Trenton hasn't heard any of the artists so far, though, so he really cannot comment on them at all. The executives know this too, knowing that he was missing for a good 45 minutes, and so he missed three of the acts already. Someone says something about him needing to focus, and this admonition falls on deaf ears. He starts to look around for the cocaine again, needing to take the edge off. Spotting it, he makes his way to the tray and helps himself to four lines before starting to scout for his second victim.

2

Across town Toni is nervous. At twenty-three, she has been doing the rounds of the local music scene, trying to land a big break. Hell, she has been trying to land any break, but it just hasn't happened yet. This has nothing to do with the fact that she is black since there has been a barrage of successful black songstresses as far back as she can remember. But it could have something to do with the uniqueness of her sound. Her tone is rich and interesting, but it really is an acquired taste.

She knows that you either like her sound, or you don't, and that is why she is more than a little anxious.

Trenton is really a force in the music industry, and she knows this. The fact that she has the opportunity to perform for him, at one of his parties, has her in a little bit of a twist. Her stomach is knotting as she changes, checks herself in the mirror, and then changes again. She doesn't want to come across as over eager, but she also doesn't want to sell her sexiness at the expense of her voice. She has heard rumors of Trenton's escapades, and so she doesn't want to give him the wrong idea.

Toni is aware of her own sexuality too. Standing naked, again, in front of the mirror, holding up a little lime dress that compliments her chocolate complexion almost too perfectly, she raises her chest a little more by breathing in. The music business is about the package, and her breasts are perfect little packages parked perfectly on her chest. She drops the dress to the floor and takes her breasts in her hands, fingering her own dark nipples. She just has great tits.

She sways her hips from side to side and then starts to gyrate her midsection in small circles, singing her planned opening number, trying to see what it is that everyone else will see when she performs. Toni thinks again as she lets out the final notes of the number, as to whether or not she should wear a bra, knowing that this is mostly not necessary, but she decides to wear one anyway. The dress that she has finally decided to go with will cover up this piece of underwear, and just cover up her thighs. She has decided to go with a cream off the shoulder mini dress, again on the compliments her complexion perfectly.

After checking her appearance just one more time, and checking again with her roommate that she looks okay, she makes her way out to her car. Butterflies start to creep into her stomach again, though, she is always nervous before a show, any show. Hoping that her car will start, she turns the key in the ignition, and fortunately, it takes on the first attempt. Thank god, she thinks, as she makes her way to the address scribbled on the back of a napkin. She remembers too the night that Cole Harris, an executive at Live Records wrote down the address after he saw her perform at a local pub.

That night had gone well, really well. She belted out the lyrics to her own compositions like a seasoned pro, completely unplugged, moving effortlessly from guitar to piano. She remembers being more comfortable with the six string that particular night too, as she always is. Something about the intimacy of the instrument really resonates with her. After her last song in the set, a deep, jazzy number about love that she had written just two days before, Cole came up to her and complimented her on her tone and her skills. He was looking too long at her breasts, so she thought there was more to his offer than just the opportunity to put her in front of some influential people. As he scribbled on the napkin too, the date and the address of the soiree, his eyes lingered over her frame. But when he hands her his business card too, a luxurious looking piece of plastic that was too beautiful to be polluted with the ink from his fountain pen, and then leaves, she thought immediately that maybe just maybe he was being genuine.

Now she was making her way to the

Malibu estate, and the butterflies in her stomach are really starting to feel like bumblebees. She knows that she not late too, since she is set to perform around 11, and so she takes it easy on the heavily congested roads. She puts on her cd player, and sings along with Nina Simone, occasionally checking the directions she got from Google. The closer she gets to the estate, though, going through boom after boom in the largely gated community, her voice is warm and ready. She, though, is a whole other story.

There are two security checkpoints upon arrival. The second and final one is the most intimidating, with the Puerto Rican security guard on the phone trying to locate Cole for fifteen full minutes. Eventually, they locate him, and only after the guard puts her on the phone with the middle-aged exec does he finally remember who she is. The nerves overcome her again, thinking that perhaps she was not as memorable to him as she had thought, and thinking that she might now not actually have the sound that they are looking for. Chin up girl, she tells herself, knowing that she is already here so she might as well get on with it, not expecting too much to come of this now after all.

She meets Cole at the front door, and he has obviously had a few drinks. After greeting him, she takes her guitar out of the boot of the beat up Honda, and hands the keys to the valet, who looks more than a little unimpressed with the vehicle. Fuck him, she whispers under her breath and follows Cole inside. He offers her a glass of champagne, which she accepts but doesn't drink. She follows him through the massive halls and into the living room, then out onto the terrace. There is quite a nice crowd gathered, but nobody paying her any sort of attention.

Cole introduces her to a few of his colleagues and whispers something about trying to find Trenton before leaving her alone in the crowd. She feels suddenly out of her depth, and she eyes the glass of bubbles in her hand. Still, she doesn't drink it, asking a waiter rather shyly for a ginger ale. It appears as if by magic, the waiter obviously sensing her discomfort and knowing that in the hierarchy of things, she and he are probably on the same level. Toni makes her way to the fringes of the crowd, and sips on her drink, speaking silently to her guitar, reassuring the instrument that this will all be over soon. Then Cole is suddenly in front of her, with an obviously wired Trenton.

"Trenton, this is the little songstress I told you about. You have got to..." he starts, Toni handing Trenton, her hand in anticipation of some acknowledgment. When she gets none she assumes that this is because her hand ends in a glass of ginger ale, the other occupied by her guitar, and so she returns the glass close to her chest. Now Trenton looks, but not at her face.

"I'm Toni," she offers up, not knowing what more she should say but feeling like there should be more.

"So, you wanna be a singer?" Trenton asks her, the sarcasm cutting through her like a scalpel.

"I am a singer!" she says, suddenly not liking him very much, and not needing to play nice. She will sing her three songs and then never have to see this smug bastard again. Toni cannot explain it, even to herself, but she really doesn't like him at all. She just wants to do what she is here to do and be done with it. Of course, she could leave at any moment, this not being a paying gig and all, but she has always treated herself like a professional. And professionals don't leave because the client is an asshole. Besides, she reminds herself that while Trenton Lively is the owner of Live Records, he is not the only decision-maker at the label. And maybe, just maybe, she can get the attention of a couple of the other executives, as she had done with Cole.

After she is shown to the stage, she makes her way onto it. There is no chance for a sound check, no chance for her to get comfortable with the acoustics of the space, everybody starting to look up at her now. She thinks of the songs she decided to sing and then looks down at the crowd. She isn't sure how her velvety tone will go down with the audience, or even if they will appreciate the lyrics. There are a couple of celebrities in the audience too, and from what she has read or heard about these people, their taste might not even allow them to understand her music. But she needs to be authentic, already resigning herself to the fact that her particular brand of authenticity might fall largely on deaf ears.

She starts to strum out a riff, almost anticipating the crowd to start booing. Instead, though, after listening to her for but a second, a second which felt like hours, they return to whatever it is they were doing, not seeming to pay her much mind at all. She wonders if they can even hear her, or if she should have started with a different song. Toni's resolve though is almost as strong as she is beautiful, and she just keeps on strumming. So what if they aren't listening. The two or three people that are watching her are enough for her to feel like she is at least performing for someone. She strums for another minute before she starts to belt out a low, husky, toasted melody of rich lyrics that mean more to her than she thinks they could ever mean to anybody else.

Toni thinks of closing her eyes, to drown out the disinterest she is seeing around her. She decides against it, though, her defiant streak surfacing again. She looks from her instrument to the audience, catching more and more people actually looking at her now. She skims the crowd, looking for Trenton. For some reason, she really wants to know if he is listening to her. She really needs him to be listening to her. If she can get the interest of the owner of the label, then that will see her cut clear through all the usual red tape that sees many an artist die by the side of the road of I-almost-made-it.

Trenton is nowhere to be seen, though, and Toni returns to her instrument. She caresses it almost, as she starts her second, and then her third song. There are no breaks in between, no need to wait for applause. She isn't sure that she will get any anyway and so she just belts on to the end. By the time she is finished with her beautiful trilogy, she takes a moment, breathes in deep with her eyes closed, and kisses the top of her guitar. This is as much to thank the instrument for having her back, as it is just to thank it for being there with her through this ordeal.

Random people start to clap, though, and she looks up. She looks around at where the clapping is coming from and bows her head in acknowledgment of this applause. Looking for the other random group, spotting it, she bows again. All too soon though the applause stop, and she gets up and removes herself from the stage. She cannot wait to get out of there, and away from all these people who wouldn't know real music if you smacked them sideways in the face with it, she thinks.

She walks off the stage, and towards the terrace door. She has stopped looking for Trenton now, and all but forgotten about Cole. All she wants is to get into her car and be gone from here. Toni gets into the living space and looks for the front door. Suddenly a little disoriented, she doesn't know which way it is. She stands in the living area just inside the terrace doors, looks around herself for somebody that she can ask for directions, a waiter, anybody. She sees nobody, though, at least not anybody that looks like they will give her the time of day.

She sees a tray of champagne flutes in the corner, and after thinking about it for a moment, she walks towards it. She grabs a glass, and looks around the space, trying to appear as though she is just taking a moment before she leaves. The artwork on the high walls in the double volume space catches her attention, and still carrying her guitar she gravitates towards it, lost almost completely in the abstract pieces that seem to be hanging away from the wall. They look like they are going to fall off the wall actually at any moment.

Cole comes up behind her and places a hand on her shoulder. It is bare, and his fingers send electrical pulses into her. This takes her by surprise, and she finishes the contents of her glass before she turns around. When she sees who it is, she relaxes a little bit, but then she realizes that he is really even more drunk now than he was when she arrived. She looks at him, waiting for him to either thank her for showing up or tell her how she blew it. He doesn't though, and just looks at her for a moment.

"That was good," he says at last.

"Thank you... I just don't think it

went down well with the audience..." Toni says, starting to make excuses for the people that really have no say as to the outcome of this sort-of-kind-of-audition.

"So, do you wanna hang around for a bit... Trenton will probably want to speak to you a little later..." Cole says, and she knows that since it is almost 2 AM, this is highly unlikely. She just needs to get out of here, and she will hear from them later if they really liked her. Toni doesn't think that she will be getting a call, though because she really doesn't think Trenton heard a single note.

"No, I think I'm gonna go... here..." Toni says, handing him a card she had printed just for this purpose. "It's late..." she puts her glass down and starts to walk in the direction of where she thinks the door is. She is obviously going the wrong way because Cole is suddenly walking out in front of her and leading the way. They get to the front door, and he opens it for Toni. He doesn't follow her outside, and she is silently grateful. She can't really stand drunk men, especially when she is sober. And Toni is way too sober to deal with what just went down at the Lively mansion.

She remembers the $100 of mad money that she has in the side zipper of her purse. This isn't like an emergency fund, which she keeps in a jar on her fridge. Instead, it is money that she uses for entertainment, usually a dinner out or a few drinks when she needs it. Right now, she really needs a drink. She gets out of Malibu and makes her way to a more affordable part of town, closer to her own apartment. She leaves her guitar in her car and makes sure she locks it up good, and then enters to not so seedy but equally dodgy pub. She is not here for the ambiance.

Toni really is consumed with thoughts of the evening now. She wonders why exactly she was invited to Malibu. Could it really have been that Cole saw something in her, and wanted to be sure? Could it just be that she was a hot woman and Cole thought that if he let her belt out a few notes, he might stick his treble clef all up in her base? She doesn't know, and she would be lying to herself if she said that she didn't care. Toni really takes her music seriously, and after trying for years to break into the industry, she thought that maybe this would be it. Clearly, it wasn't because everyone that was supposed to pay attention to her seemed more interested in the contents of their glasses and the white powder that lined their noses rather conspicuously.

After ordering a double vodka and cranberry juice, Toni finds her way into the corner, a vantage point that allows her to watch the other patrons without being seen herself. She loves watching people, drawing inspiration for her songs from the things people do and say, and also the things that they don't do, and don't say. People watching is a habit that she developed just before she dropped out of college. She would sit and watch everyone else who could afford to stay there, who lived so nonchalantly thanks to the support of their parents, and really wished that she was any of them. She really wished that she could, for the duration of her studies at least, be anybody but herself.

But now she is here, four years into her music hustle, and getting nowhere.

She sips on her drink and watches the groups of people, so different from the Malibu crowd, but equally oblivious of her presence. Toni isn't insecure, by no means. She knows that she can sing, and she knows too that she is incredibly beautiful. She has been told this often enough to really believe it now. But her voice and beauty have really done little to move her up the musical food chain, she has never found herself in that all elusive right place at the right time.

Toni doesn't notice the drink placed down in front of her. Her eyes are fixed on the group of Goths in the corner, near the door. The groups seem rather androgynous, and she is unable to tell to tell the guys from the girls. They are really beautiful, though, and Toni finds herself strangely drawn to them. She toys with the idea of being a Goth too, thinking that this is the perfect way for her to hide from her reality and escape from herself for moments of time, at least.

Long fingers move the glass in front of her, and this movement draws her attention for a moment. Her eyes rest on the fingers, and then on the thick dark wrist. Perfectly formed forearms are attached to the wrists, and they become the most incredible biceps. When he gets passed the thick neck, and to his perfectly chiseled face, her attention is finally shifted from the Goths. She smiles in response to the smile that is coming down off the stranger's handsome face.

"Lamar..." he says, letting go of the glass and extending a hand to her.

"Toni," she says, taking his hand, surprised by the coldness of the fingers for a moment but then remembering that they were just seconds earlier wrapped around the chilled glass.

"May I?" he asks, pulling a chair closer to the table where she was more than a little comfortable alone.

"Sure," she says, thinking that this man might just be the perfect distraction from this night's affairs. It is almost 4 AM now, though, and Toni really thinks that it is perhaps time for her to leave. But she will entertain him briefly, half an hour at the most.

It is almost 5 though when she realizes that she has actually laughed more in the last while than she has in a long time. She isn't tired, though, but she does feel that she needs to get home. Toni starts to think of what she can say to make her getaway, but she really doesn't want to. Lamar isn't the usual clean cut guy that she would go for, but as far as one night stands go, he is definitely not to be scoffed at. He hasn't said anything though that lets her know that he wants to enjoy anything but her company.

Maybe he is shy, she thinks, but then again so is she. She has never been the aggressor, not in relationships, and certainly not in the art of casual sexual encounters. She has had a few, so she is not totally against the idea of random NSA action. But she has neither the words nor the wherewithal to even suggest that they go back to her place, or his. It's a Thursday morning too, so she doesn't know what plans he has for the day, or if he has to go to work. She has the whole day before her usual gig that night at the Purple Dragoon, a local club for wannabe singers.

She decides that this is too complicated for her, and so after she downs her drink she gets up. She says her goodbyes and hands Lamar, her hand. He holds it for the longest time, not wanting her to leave. He asks her a million questions with his eyes, and she just looks at her watch, letting him know that she really thinks that it is time for her to get going. Still, he holds her hand, caressing the top of it, playing with her fingers. She thinks that at last, he is getting to the point.

Again Toni just smiles at him and pulls her hand away. Lamar gets up and lingers with his eyes on her breasts for the slightest moment. Then she turns away from him, saying goodbye again with her back to him. This time his eyes fall on her ass, and the place where the dress suddenly becomes her thick beautiful thighs. She really isn't thinking of a relationship. All she knows is that she really enjoyed his company. He too has something a little more casual in mind, but he isn't sure how receptive she will be to this advance.

He watches her walk away, and after thinking about it for the shortest time, he starts to follow her out. She gets to the door, Lamar in tow, but she hasn't seen him. Then she gets to the street and walks to where she parked, feeling eyes on her, but not looking back at all. As she unlocks her car a hand suddenly envelops hers and turns the key. She recognizes those fingers, and she smiles to herself. This is the perfect end to a not so perfect evening, she thinks to herself if Lamar is any good in bed.

Hell even if he is not so good, she doesn't really care. It has been a minute since she was in the presence of a naked man, and she really just needs to pounding anonymity of no-strings-attached sexual play. As long as it isn't an experiment, as long as Lamar isn't a virgin, then whatever he brings will do just nicely. They will go back to her place she thinks, just so that she is comfortable with her surroundings.

They get in the car and drive the few blocks to her apartment building. The space between her thighs warms at the prospect of Lamar, especially when she steals a glimpse of his package, bulging already between his thighs. It is an impressive piece of meat, and so she relaxes into the fact that she will certainly not have to be faking anything tonight. As it grows a little more the excitement gives way to nerves, though, as she remembers that it really has been a while since she was last fucked, and unlike riding a bike, you need to be rather wet if you are going to have any hope of enjoying the penetration.

3

Lamar doesn't even try to hide his erection as the walk into the building and up the stairs to Toni's apartment. He cannot keep his hands off Toni though and keeps his fingers running up and down the small of her back. Then he slips down onto her ass, and she doesn't flinch. He knows now that she is in it with him, and that she will probably let him take the reins on this morning's proceedings. The sun has started to come up now, and so when they get to the apartment and open the door, both Toni and Lamar are very glad for the thick drapes that keep the sunlight out.

Toni isn't sure if she should offer him a drink, but when thoughts of the previous night start to creep up on her, thoughts of Cole, and especially thoughts of a rather nonchalant Trenton, she decides against it. Why this is still bothering her though she doesn't know, but she knows one thing, that Lamar will offer up a significant enough distraction if she can just make quick work of her dress and his trousers.

She doesn't need to worry too much about undressing him, though because as soon as she has locked the door, he starts to undress himself. She wants to watch it, to see what exactly she is in store for, but instead she lifts her own dress up over her shoulders and head and drops it to the floor. Then she takes off her panties, before Lamar has got to his boxers, and she stands naked while he slowly removes his shorts, almost as though he were performing for her a little.

When she leads the way to the bedroom, Lamar follows her, albeit slowly. She gets to the bedroom, and he is still walking down the hallway.

Toni hasn't even kissed him yet, and so she starts to ask herself all the standard pre-one-night-stand questions that she usually does. Before she can answer them though he is standing in the doorway. His fingers take hold of his cock, and its thickness is almost amplified. As he moves his fingers up and down his shaft, the length seems to be augmented. He starts to tug on his balls, and even these orbs seem abnormally large.

He comes closer to her, and she realizes that nothing about his anatomy is exaggerated. He really does have an enormous cock and really large balls. She likes it, but she is definitely not even going to try and suck on the monstrosity. Also, she looks at her bedside clock and realizes the time, knowing that she really wants to get this party started. Thoughts of Trenton start to come up in her head again, and she really needs to get this going now. She has no idea why she is thinking of Trenton at all by the way, but with the prospect of what is about to go down, she quickly shifts focus.

Lamar comes up to her and holds her face in both his large hands. She lets him pull her up towards him, and as she goes onto her tiptoes she lets her lips fall on his, or his on hers, she cannot be sure. She waits to see if he can kiss, and when he parts her lips with his tongue and takes her tongue in his, she knows for sure that he can. He kisses her the way she likes to be kissed, and so she kisses him right back.

Their tongues lock in a beautiful dance, and Lamar effortlessly lifts Toni off the floor. He walks them over to the bed and lays both of them down on it, still joined at the mouth. They keep on kissing, and Lamar starts to rub his penis against her clit. It is totally unplanned too, there is just nowhere else for this mammoth dick to go. He starts to grind his erection against her, and it gets thicker and longer with every movement. She starts to wonder if she will be able to take it.

He pulls his mouth off hers and looks at her in her eyes. She returns his gaze, not sure of the question that he is asking her with his eyes. Then he kisses her neck and turns her over with just one hand. On her stomach now, she wonders what he is up to. He is still kissing her neck, though, so she lets herself go in the moment. Then he starts to kiss her all the way up and down her back and then settles on the small of her back with his thick full lips.

Lamar literally massages her lower back with his lips. He lets his tongue leave his mouth too now, and settles this in the space just above her crack. She really wishes that he can just get on with it, but she cannot hide the fact that she is enjoying it. She doesn't even look at the clock anymore. If he has anywhere to be that really is his problem. She doesn't need to be anywhere for at least fourteen hours. Toni decides to relax into it and just enjoy the attention. Thoughts of Trenton still creep up on her, but then Lamar's lips and tongue pull her back into the moment.

His thick fingers dig into her lower back too now, and then the tips of his fingers work their way onto her ass cheeks. She starts to think that this is going where she hopes, and it is, but not just yet. After pummeling her ass cheeks with his digits, he pulls them apart. Instead of landing his tongue on her cunt from the back, though, which is really what she had hoped for, he licks her asshole tenderly. In fact, so tender are his licks that she raises her ass into his mouth now.

Then he starts to snake his tongue inside her ass, and she suddenly pulls away. She has never had her ass rimmed before, and for a black brother to be doing this is even more surprising to her. But Lamar really seems to be enjoying himself, because he lifts her ass up to his mouth now, and digs his tongue in deeper. Toni isn't sure what she tastes like, she isn't sure if this is even appropriate. She has never had this done to her before, and so she is more than a little confused.

Slowly though she starts to surrender to this happening, and then she is really in it. She starts to grind against his grip, really feeding him her ass. He goes deeper and deeper into her asshole with his tongue, and when it does finally give way completely, he is fucking her ass with his hot, thick tongue. He wets her asshole so completely that his tongue starts to move easier and easier into her, and he really goes for it a little more. Deeper and deeper he digs into her, and he seems to almost forget that there are other parts of her that are craving attention too now.

When he pulls his tongue from her, she wants it back in her immediately. However, her cunt is so warm and wet too now, and aching somewhat deep inside so that she knows that she really wants him to pay some homage to her pussy too. She lifts her ass some more, hoping that he takes the hint, but he doesn't. He goes into her asshole again and fucks her more than a little aggressively now, eating her ass out with an intensity that has her practically shivering from the pleasure now.

Lamar lifts her ass himself now, pulling her up to her knees. He sticks his nose where his tongue just was, and the feeling of his nose in her wet ass feels a little uncomfortable too now. Then he removes it, and extends his tongue out and onto her pussy. He parts her lips with his tongue and licks the entrance to her pussy rather gently. As he enters her pussy with his tongue, though, his gentleness subsides. He tongue-fucks her cunt hard, and she feels like she could have an orgasm at any moment now.

He holds her in place, bringing her higher up on her knees now, and digging deeper into her with his tongue. He manages to pull her back from the brink of climax, and then guide her gently towards it again with just his tongue. Over and over again he handles her cunt expertly with his tongue until she feels like she is on a seesaw of almost climaxes, one that drives her so insane she starts to feel like she is actually on a merry-go-round. Time is suddenly irrelevant to Toni, and it seems to be totally irrelevant to Lamar as well.

Then he pulls his tongue from her and digs it back into her ass again. He goes into her asshole aggressively and fucks her with his tongue for the longest while. Then he pulls the tongue from her ass, and as she falls to the bed, he digs his fingers into her lower back again. He works his fingers up her back to her shoulders. He massages her shoulders so deeply and so well that Toni relaxes even more into what was supposed to be a one-night stand but is turning into the best sex that she has had in a while. And they haven't even started fucking yet.

He gets up suddenly and leaves the room. Toni looks around for him, coming out of the daze that she is in a little bit. Lamar returns to the room and finishes rolling the condom down over his length. She knows that the condoms in her side drawer that she kept for emergencies would probably not even have fitted him anyway. He probably knew that she would have the XXL required by his humongous tool either, so she is glad, as is he, that he is prepared.

Lamar jumps back onto the bed, and after massaging her back a little longer, he turns her over. He works his hands up and down her belly, and then onto her breasts. He takes her nipples between his fingers and turns them gently. Then he holds the full breast in his hand and squeezes as gently, then a little harder. He makes his way down her belly again and finds her clit with his finger. Lamar works on her clit for a moment and then slips his finger between her cunt lips, entering her very slowly. He doesn't even look at her now, watching his own hand as his finger disappears inside her.

He fingers her deliciously slowly with just this finger, and Toni closes her eyes. He builds up to two, and then three fingers and she really starts to feel the stretch. Then she starts to moan, loudly, as he parts these fingers the deeper they go, bringing them back together as he pulls them partially out. She gets what he is doing at last, and throws her eyes down to where his python is a menacing cock now, stiff and ready to assault her tightness as soon as he feels she is ready.

Her pussy is wet, and then even wetter as she has a mild orgasm. He is in no hurry, patiently waiting for just the right time to mount her, just the right time to snake his way inside her. He thinks that she might be ready now too, because he is slowly removing his fingers from her now, and positioning her on her back, parting her legs and making his way between them. He is on his knees, bending down to her, kissing her belly, and then sucking gently on her breasts. He knows that his cock is big, and he probably knows that this has been a problem for him before, so he is really not about to just ram it into her and go for gold.

Then he kisses his way up her belly and settles on her neck. He kisses her neck tenderly while rubbing his cock against her clit. Then he moves up and places the head of his cock between her lips. He starts to move it up and down, not really going in, not forcing it into her, just teasing her cunt with his thickness. She braces herself every time he seems like he is going to go in, but then he doesn't, just parting her lips more with his head, almost as though he is testing the waters.

Lamar is very slow, very deliberate, and Toni almost feels the need to scream for him to get on with it. But she doesn't rush him in any way, knowing that when he does go for it, no doubt it's going to be quite a stretch. Then he starts to enter her, and she is more than a little overwhelmed. This is partly due to the fact that it really has been a while since she last got some, but also just because Lamar really is quite a remarkable size. He eases himself into her slowly, but not slow enough, and Toni holds her breath.

With half of him inside her, he starts to thrust gently. Then he eases a little more of himself into her, and still, she holds her breath a little more. When she breathes in, he manages just a little bit more of himself into her, and then he stops moving completely. Then he starts to thrust inside her, slowly, deliciously, and she tries to relax rather quickly to get him comfortable. She also starts moaning loudly, and this has everything to do with the ramrod being driven into her right now. As soon as she starts to relax a little more, though, she realizes that her cunt is wetting itself enough to accommodate the invasion.

Toni has only ever slept with black guys before, and so she knows the size of their meat. Lamar really is bigger than most, though, and he is probably the biggest that she has ever had, but she is really starting to enjoy it. She starts to grind against him, but not too enthusiastically, not wanting him to send more of himself inside her. She doesn't think that she can take more of him, and so she just keeps him where he is just so that she can make the necessary adjustments within herself.

He fucks her deliciously, though, with just about two-thirds of his cock, and she really starts to enjoy it. She still doesn't move too much, though, really not wanting to upset this rhythm that they have established. Lamar also seems to be resigned to the parts of her that she has let him have, and he just keeps thrusting into her with an almost sincere determination. Toni relaxed when she realizes that Lamar isn't going to go any deeper, and Lamar really enjoys the parts of her that he is moving freer around right now.

Lamar starts to thrust a little harder, just a little deeper, Toni not moving at all again. She is feeling the pleasure of each and every stroke, but still, she is feeling the tension of being impaled by Lamar. She breathes in a little deeper and then lets out a long moan, so loud that even she is caught by surprise. Lamar just keeps on thrusting into her, though, easy and almost too controlled. This control slips a little, and he loses himself a little further into her pussy, almost breaking through the tightness that he finds deeper inside her.

She starts to feel the beginnings of an orgasm, and she lets herself go towards this beautiful light. Worrying too much about Lamar now is impossible because she starts to lose herself in her own pleasure. Even as Lamar inches a little deeper into her, she lets him, just moaning, and then murmuring louder and louder. He starts to grunt too now, deep and really bassy so that she knows that he too is getting very close. She didn't expect them to cum together, and even when they do she still half doesn't believe it. He really has learned to work with his massive tool.

Toni is satisfied, more than she believed that she would be. He took his time on her, and as she throws her eyes to her bedside clock and realizes just how much time. It is almost 11, and she is sweating from every part of her. She doesn't want this to be awkward now, doesn't want the standard shame that usually follows all her one night stands. At least though she will not be the one doing the walk of shame, not this time. Lamar just has to leave her to her shower and bed, and that will be that.

Fortunately, he seems to understand the workings of the one nighter. He thrusts into her a few more times for good measure and then eases his way out of her cunt. He drops a few more kisses on her neck and then one full on her lips. Then he gets up and sorts out his cock, still hard, but dripping with excessive cum into the condom. He looks around for the bathroom, and after she gives him the general layout of the apartment, he disappears through her bedroom door, leaving her alone with her thoughts and her incredible satisfaction.

When Lamar reappears in the doorway, he is fully clothed. She has a robe on and is busying herself with nothing, in particular, opening and then closing, and then reopening her drapes. They say their goodbyes as she walks him to the front door. He kisses her again, and there is that awkward moment where he doesn't know if he should ask her for her number. He doesn't though, saying that he will see her around before he turns int0 the hallway and walks down towards the elevator. She locks herself in and makes the way to the bathroom.

She lies in the bath, the hot water still running slowly into the tub. As the water covers her pussy, she touches herself with her fingers, tenderly. Her cunt really is feeling more delicate than she expected, but she really doesn't worry too much about this. It was good. It was fucking awesome. Actually, she tells herself, watching the water etch up her belly and over her breasts. She reaches for the faucet and closes the hot water now, moving the liquid around herself trying to dilute hot and cold. She makes a mental not to use her next bit of mad money on bubble bath.

Toni thinks about Lamar for a moment, thinking that perhaps she could have been more active during their session. She knows though that this was impossible, the first round dedicated solely to the adjustment. It wasn't an altogether bad adjustment either, she tells herself, and so she dismisses the thought. She does wonder if she will see him again, though, perhaps for a rematch. The woman inside her really wants a rematch. She knows that she is not as boring as she must have come across to Lamar. But he came, and so did she, and so she can pack the experience away in her very small box of such experiences and move on to other thoughts.

A thought that she didn't expect to have though is of Trenton. She doesn't know why, but she suddenly really wonders why he didn't seem at all interested in her music last night. Perhaps she isn't what he is looking for, and so she tries to dismiss this thought from her. It doesn't let go, though, tugging at her like a nagging child on his mother's skirt. She has had gigs before, most of them nonpaying, so why was this one different? Perhaps she had already allowed herself to believe that at last, it was going to happen for her.

A recording contract with Live Records will really change her life. It will mean that she gets out of this cramped apartment and moves a little closer to Hollywood. She really wants to be in the thick of LA society, and even if her address isn't Beverly Hills or Malibu, anywhere but here would be an improvement. She bites her lip as she allows herself to daydream of what a recording deal would mean for her.

Not only would her address improve, but also her artistic freedom. She would be able to get into the Studio, really get in there, and make music. Not that she isn't making music now, and not that she isn't churning out new songs like an ice-cream maker. But there is a freedom that comes with money, a freedom that says that you do not have to worry about whether or not you can afford shampoo, and where champagne will be your drink of choice, not your drink of 'oh yeah bitch, you wish...'

She sinks into the tub and lets the water cover her hair. At least she doesn't need to worry about a weave because well, she doesn't have one. Her hair is as natural as it is going to get, as natural as it can be given the little bit of relaxer she has combed through it. She cannot even remember when she did the treatment, but it was one of the home treatments that left you wondering if you had done it right. It was good enough for her current life, though. Toni imagines what it will feel like to have a real weave put in one day, or even if she wants one.

After coming back up to the surface of the water, she again makes for her cunt with her fingers. She goes into herself with the tips of two of her digits, trying to break herself away from daydreaming about weaves and champagne. She thinks that it is just wishful thinking anyway, and so it will really do her no good to think of such things. Her cunt aches a little, just a little now, and so she goes deeper into herself with her fingers. She will bring herself to another orgasm before she finishes her bath and wraps herself in bed.

Digging into her pussy seems familiar to her, too familiar. Even with the recent sex that she just had, less than an hour ago, this familiarity seems somehow necessary. She knows even that this orgasm will be ten, maybe twenty times better than the one brought on by Lamar. She knows herself, and she knows her body. She knows what gets her off. So she closes her eyes and goes to that place where she is fucked, no, made love to, by the man of her dreams.

In her fantasies, before this, they have always been black men, with large penises, not uncomfortably large, though, not like Lamar. But they have been big enough to reach her depths while being all up in her business. She gets close to blowing, and suddenly an image of a man comes into her head, clear as though he were right there in the bathtub with her. She stops moving her fingers inside herself and literally shakes her head free of the images of Trenton. Why would she be thinking of Trenton?

As she goes into herself again, she goes through various versions of the alpha African American male again, but again Trenton creeps up on her. Eventually, she just gives in, allowing her imagination to undress him, to let her know, at least in her head what his lips feel like. To give him a perfectly circumcised dick, not to large, but certainly not small, and move in and out of her with as much urgency as tenderness. She really imagines him in incredible detail, but she also knows, as she cums, that she really has no frame of reference for this man who never really even spoke to her at all. Toni feels strangely dirty for even thinking this, and even more so for getting off on thoughts of Trenton Lively.

4

Toni is not the only one who has her head on someone that she never thought possible. Trenton too is really obsessing about Toni too, and it is not because of her voice. He remembers the dress that she wore last night, the cream, and how if became her dark chocolate thighs a moment too soon. Was she trying to get his attention, because if she was, it really worked? He has had his cock sucked by three women since Toni appeared at his house hours earlier, but still, she is the only woman on his mind.

It is just after 12 noon, and he is yet to sleep. He walks from his bedroom to the kitchen, quite a stretch, pulling on his cock, not quite hard, not quite soft. Cocaine has that effect on his cock, as it does everybody's Trenton knows. But at least it does nothing to reduce his size, and he pulls on the head a little harder. Then he takes his fingers to his balls, tugging on them as he walks into the kitchen, needing some orange juice.

He pulls the orange juice from the fridge and walks naked onto his terrace. Some staff members are at the house, cleaning up after the night's event, but he doesn't care. They don't seem to mind either, mostly ignoring the naked white man with the long cock. Trenton feels the urge to have more cocaine, but he knows better. He isn't an addict, and really just does it recreationally. But he knows that he is playing with fire if he decides to start doing it on his own. Instead, he takes a gulp of orange juice and then throws himself into the swimming pool.

As he does a few laps, mostly underwater, his thoughts turn again to Toni. She had the best tits he has seen on a woman in a while, and he doesn't even like black girls. Or does he, he wonders. He comes up over the edge of the water and looks over the rim flow at the ocean just beyond. He thinks that perhaps he just never thought to explore this, or is it that black women have just always been out of his reach. They have never shown him any interest, and this starts to eat away at his ego.

He ducks his head under the water and then lifts himself out of the pool completely. Wet, he stands near the balustrade on the terrace and watches the people filtering onto the beach. Some of them look up at him and don't even skip a beat at his nakedness. He doesn't mind the eyes either, running a few fingers over his cock again. This isn't even to lure them in, or to get them to look a little longer. He just has thoughts of Toni floating around in his head, and he starts to wonder what her mouth might feel like on his cock. Suddenly he starts to harden.

Trenton looks around him, staff still moving around the bottom story of his house. He looks down at his growing erection and tries to cover it with his hands. It takes both of them to cover his tool, but it is obvious from how he is holding it that it is really hard now.

He walks to the pool house, which is the closest retreat to where he is almost in view of the servants trickling onto the terrace now. After a quick duck into the cottage, he closes and locks the door. To say that he is relieved is a massive understatement.

He closes the drapes and lies on the couch. For no reason at all, he turns on the TV that is mounted on the wall, and turns up the volume, again for no apparent reason. Trenton holds his cock firmer now and runs his fingers up and down the length of his shaft. It is impressive, but he has newfound insecurities now, as he compares his cock to the imagined length of his black counterparts. He can't remember ever seeing a black man's dick either, but his imagination is really playing tricks on him. After wetting his fingers in his mouth, he takes hold of his cock again and tries to shake the images of black meat from his head.

The black meat that he tries to focus on is Toni's though. Shit, she is really one fine piece of woman. He knows too that she has a voice, and he starts to form a plan in his head about how he can see her again. Fortunately, Cole is the one who discovered her so it won't take too much convincing for them to sign her. As the plan to sign her fully develops in his head, his erection forms to its fullness in his hand. He starts to stroke his cock from the base to the tip, watching his fingers moving with deliberate slowness over his long thick tool.

Trenton closes his eyes now, needing to imagine that it was Toni's fingers moving on him now. Still, it doesn't work, though. He swaps hands, using his left hand because of the unfamiliarity of this handling. He wets his left fingers with a lot more saliva than he did his right, and this works even better. Trenton starts to get into it now, building a rhythm, and getting himself into the preemptive motions of climax.

He moves lower on the couch so that he is almost lying down now. Pulling his cock away from his naval, so that it points to the ceiling. The tension that this creates in his dick serves him very well indeed. He pulls on the head, then a few inches underneath it. Then he pulls on these few inches including the head and keeps on tugging, harder and harder. Again he works his fingers down to the base of his tool and works on the whole shaft. He wets the fingers on his right hand and starts to pull on his balls hard too, completing his pleasure circuit.

All time is lost now, no urgency at all for him to be anywhere. He never goes into the office on a Thursday, or any other day that he doesn't feel like it, and he knows that this is wrong. His inheritance has served him well up until now, though, and he has a really competent staff, so he doesn't feel the need to mess with the wheel. If it ain't broke, he figures, then it just ain't broke.

Trenton really starts to focus on the hands moving up and down his cock now, and on his balls, squeezing deeper and harder on his cock, and pulling really hard on his balls now. He squeezes his nuts too, really getting his fingers in there, and then pulls on the soft flesh of the sack. His eyes are closed so tightly now that he starts to tear, his teeth parted by his tongue as it moves over his lips. He licks his lips a lot and starts to salivate from the corner of his mouth too. The gum in his mouth probably has something to do with this, though.

He brings himself within seconds of cumming, but he doesn't. His body doesn't seem to be cooperating with him, and he seems to be retreating from orgasm now. He pulls harder on his cock, trying to will himself to climax, but again he falls just a few seconds short. After attempting three more times, he lets out a loud scream and pulls his hands away from his cock. Fuck, this is really frustrating.

He takes to his cock again, slowly this time. His erection isn't going anywhere, though, so he relaxes a little bit, but he really needs to cum. More slowly now, more deliberately he pulls on his cock. He completely ignores his balls for the moment, not knowing what is keeping him from shooting his load. Slowly, ever so slowly he moves his fingers up and down the full length of his shaft, and then after he has settled into this new rhythm, he ever so lightly feathers his balls. As he starts to feel his cock pulsating with the promise of an orgasm, he doesn't change a single thing.

At last, he feels that he might blow,

but he doesn't want to jinx it. He doesn't even try to imagine Toni naked anymore, just focusing on what he knows about her. Her tits are perfect. Her thighs are perfect. Her neck is long and beautiful. And her lips. Her lips are the delicious color of blackberries, or at least they were last night. He takes his mind's eye to her eyes too, beautiful almonds that sit almost too perfectly on her face. Yes, yes, this is what will get him over the edge. This is exactly what gets him over.

He starts to shoot his load, a long stream of heated cum initially, and then shorter squirts. These squirts land on his chest, and then his stomach, and finally a few drops settle in his pubic hair. The initial stream just missed his face and lands on the couch beside his head. He has always been impressed with his shot, showing off almost at times, when he hasn't cum into the mouths of his victims. Trenton shakes a little, then he shakes a lot, still pulling on his softening cock, squeezing the remainder of semen out of himself.

Trenton goes to the bathroom and stands under the shower. He wraps a towel around himself without drying himself off and takes some toilet paper to go and clean up the mess that he made, knowing that it will not be completely cleaned. But the staff will make their way to the pool house soon enough, so he doesn't really care. He walks out of the pool house, leaving the TV still playing, still loud. He goes to the kitchen again and takes a bottle of champagne from the fridge, taking it with him upstairs to his now clean bedroom.

He closes his bedroom door and lets the towel drop to the floor. He goes over to his bed, throws himself on it, and opens the bottle of bubbles. Turning the TV in his room on now, he sips the champagne straight out of the bottle and flips through the cartoon channels. He really hasn't got Toni out of his system yet, and he wonders why. Surely she isn't the type of woman that he would normally be attracted to. Surely he has only ever noticed lighter skinned black women before.

He has never thought of himself as racist. He knows that he isn't in fact. Why then has this thought never crossed his mind before? This really nags at him, really starts to work on him, and he is more certain now that it is because of Toni. She has opened up a cage, a Pandora 's Box of curiosity in him that he has no control over. And he really wants to explore this curiosity, but he isn't sure if it is only just with Toni. He needs to know, and he thinks he knows how to be sure of what have started to feel like real feelings.

It has only been one day, one day since he saw Toni. He cannot even say that he met her because he was drunk and wired with he did. He needs to get to the bottom of what he is feeling, and he needs to do it today. The sense of urgency overcomes him, overwhelms him almost completely, and he picks up his phone, not even realizing that he has gone through half the bottle of champagne already. He scrolls the internet on his mobile, looking for escort services with pictures. Finally, he finds what he is looking for.

A duo of escorts, one Black, the other Russian, advertise their services as 'a real Oreo experience...' Trenton dials the number on the ad, and after a brief discussion with a girl who really does sound Russian, the appointment is booked for later that afternoon. He thinks to cancel, wonders why he is feeling this way but decides to go for it anyway. If nothing else, at least he will have two first time experiences in one. He takes his cock in his hand another time, just to warm himself up, and to empty his dick out so that the experience lasts a little bit longer than usual. He will need to stay hard enough to satisfy both women, or be satisfied by them, or both. His ego couldn't handle it if he couldn't.

After a quick shower, he goes downstairs to get a few more bottles of champagne, and glasses. He also gets an ashtray, realizing that he hasn't smoked at all today, very strange for him. He opens the doors leading to the balcony of his bedroom and lights up. He goes to smoke on the balcony and waits for his escorts to arrive. After three cigarettes he goes back inside and throws on shorts, hearing the doorbell ringing downstairs, knowing that someone will get it, but knowing too that he needs to meet the women downstairs so that they are not delivered to him like women to a harem. Although, that is exactly what his bedroom has started to feel like over the last couple of months.

He gets halfway down the staircase when one of his maids shows the two women into the living area. The maid sees him and looks up to him. Trenton nods her off, and she leaves the two women, every bit as stunning as their pictures, much to his relief, and he waves his hand, ushering the women upstairs. They greet him when they eventually get to him, hugging him and kissing him on both cheeks, or rather letting him kiss them. They really are the top end of a rather seedy market. Trenton likes this.

They get to his bedroom, and he goes immediately for the champagne. He has agreed to pay them for the whole afternoon, and the entire evening, although he isn't sure if this escapade will last that long. Anyway, he has them booked, just in case. He hands them both a glass, and they clink their glasses together, before both going for his glass. The conversation flows easily, and Trenton is more than a little comfortable. The few times that he has solicited the work of prostitutes it has really just been a quick in quick out. There was no need for words or lengthy conversations about each other's lives. So he finds this tag team quite refreshing.

After getting a couple of glasses of champagne in them the girls slip out of their dresses. Trenton is really enjoying the conversation, though, so he makes a call downstairs, and as if by magic a tray of fruit and canapés is brought upstairs. By the time the tray gets to them, they have gone through two bottles of champagne, Trenton starting to feel a little frisky now, and pulling off his shorts. After two more bottles of champagne are brought upstairs in ice buckets, he locks the door unnecessarily. Nobody will ever dare to come into his bedroom unannounced. To Trenton's immense satisfaction too, the two women take to the tray like a hobo to a cheeseburger, and the black diamond in the room opens another bottle of champagne.

The Russian girl calls herself Katinka, and Trenton knows that this is probably not her real name. The Black girl calls herself, rather predictably but more believably,

Tashana, Tash for short. He presumptuously calls Katinka Kat, which seems to go down well with her, or just over her head. Since it isn't her real name anyway, she doesn't mind how he manipulates the syllables. Trenton rubs his fingers along his still soft cock and watches the women get out of their panties. Both of them are not wearing any bras. They really, really don't need them.

His focus is on Kat, though, and he goes forward, taking her nipple between two of his fingers, gauging her response, squeezing the nipple tenderly between his fingers. The look on her face is extremely erotic but somehow rehearsed. Trenton doesn't care, though, taking the nipple on the other breast between his two other fingers on his now-free hand. He squeezes a little harder, and her eyes close slowly. There is something about the look on her face though that sends the blood straight to his cock and it is hard very quickly. He looks at his cock and smiles, both women looking at his rather impressive cock now.

Kat goes down on her knees, slowly, again looking very rehearsed. But as soon as she wraps her mouth around his cock he doesn't care about this act. They probably have a whole act planned for this afternoon and evening, so he knows that he needs to just get comfortable with this performance. She slides almost all of him into her mouth, and he is more than a little impressed. She slowly releases the cock from her jaw as Tash slowly makes her way to her knees. Trenton watches her closely now, wanting to see how she is going to handle his meat.

She sucks on just the head, for the longest time. She really seems to enjoy it too, which he likes. He wants to ask her to pull on his balls, but he just decides to wait and see what she is going to do. She starts to work his cock into her mouth, and like Kat, gets it all in there, right down to the balls. Kat positions herself underneath him now, and while her partner in crime sucks on his cock, she nibbles on his nut sack. He really, really, really likes it.

They make a delicious meal of his cock too, and after about fifteen minutes Trenton feels the beginnings of an orgasm. He really does feel like he is going to blow now, and he wants to pull his dick away from their mouths. He can't though, enjoying it too much. But then, just before he sprays the contents of his cock into their mouths and on their faces, both women remove their mouths from his cock almost too suddenly, and he thrusts into the air for a moment.

He looks for their mouths again and doesn't find them where he hoped they would be. Both women are standing up, slow and sensual, and their mouths are suddenly on either one of his nipples. He takes their heads in his hands and pushes them down on his chest. They suck hard, harder than expected, and he likes it. The kisses they drop on his chest are not so hard, though, just gentle touching of their lips to the skin on the surface of his smooth front. They are suddenly off his chest, sipping on their champagne flutes again, their lips now lingering on the rim of their glasses.

Trenton decides to test his scattered theory about black females, and he pulls Tash to the bed with him. Kat watches, and follows them to the bed, more than willing to take a supporting role for this first round. He pulls the side drawer open and takes out a strip of condoms. He rolls on over his cock, still hard, so females are obviously just females with him. But then again, he knew this. Insecurity, however, starts to filter through the alcohol. He starts to think of black men working the shit out of this pussy that he has paid for, and doing it for free, for the sheer pleasure that it gave her, and them. Still, though, he has a raging hard on, and he will use it on Tash, to see if her pussy tastes any sweeter than Kat's, who he knows he will fuck in a minute.

He doesn't kiss her, doesn't do anything that vaguely resembles romance. The transactional nature of this encounter doesn't allow him to do this. He sends a finger into her neatly shaven pussy and fingers her wet for a while. Then he starts to enter her with his cock, thrusting gently into her, and then not so gently. He goes deep, all the way into her, and it is wonderful. He takes her nipple into his mouth, almost needing to double over to do so, but keeping his cock moving in and out of her. Shit her pussy is tight. It wraps so beautifully around his cock that the condom seems to disappear. There is no difference between this pussy and any other pussy he has had. No difference except for the Tash twists that she adds. He knows now once and for all that pussy is pussy, and it is up to the woman to add her own secret herbs and spices.

Trenton really enjoys Tash, really he does. He proceeds to enjoy Kat too, and even he is impressed with his stamina. At 38 he isn't old, but he is no 23-year old either. He goes round after round, and when he finally passes out, part exhaustion and a large part the five bottles of champagne he polished mostly by himself, he goes to sleep a very satisfied man. The women don't sleep, though, just finishing off the canapés and champagne and then relaxing in his hot tub. When he wakes up the next morning, the women are nowhere to be seen, and he is glad. One thing he is certain of, you really get what you pay for with high-end call girls.

He is remarkably well rested too, and his head isn't pounding for a change. So clear is his head too, that the one woman floating around in his head must be there for a reason. Toni really made an impression on him. She had really started to get under his skin, and her voice wasn't half bad either. Actually, this morning he finds himself really reminiscing about her voice. He had heard her singing, and it was a mind altering experience, even though his mind was a little bit altered when he heard her. This is a very good thing, he thinks.

Trenton decides to go into the office today, to discuss Toni. He wants to see her again, for more reasons than just her looks. He knows that he has never really shown interest in the business, but now he is. Everyone at the office will have to just deal with it, once they get over the surprise of course. He makes a call to the label on his way there and by the time he gets to the building that houses Live Records Cole is already waiting for him with a few other executives in the boardroom.

He immediately expresses interest in Toni, and rightfully says that they have nobody like her in their stable yet. Everyone is in agreement, and Cole arranges a meeting with Toni after finding her number with a simple Facebook search. He cannot remember what he did with the card that she gave him. He actually doesn't even remember if she had given him a card, although he knows that if she is any bit serious about making it in the business, she would have had them at the ready for him, or anyone for that matter who showed interest in her.

After a few meetings, Toni is excited about receiving the call that she really wasn't sure she was going to get. They want to sign her, and she really wants to sign. She makes a note not to sign anything though until she has had a lawyer look at it. But as she gets ready for the first day at Live Records, the first meeting with Trenton since the party, she is nervous, dressing in jeans, just so that she can be sure that the contract really isn't just about her beautifully toned legs.

5

Trenton is nervous. Actually, he is sober, and this makes him appear nervous and uneasy. He has a t-shirt and jeans on, and sandals, looking every bit like a music executive, not! He doesn't take his life seriously. He hasn't taken his life seriously until now. But there is something about Toni that makes him want to be sober, and present for this meeting. He paces his office and starts to look around the space that he hasn't really spent nearly enough time in.

Cole comes in and looks at him, up and down. Cole is either seriously overdressed, or Trenton is remarkably underdressed. No prize for guessing which it is. He picks up the letter opener and looks at Cole standing in his doorway. He wants to ask him a million questions about Toni, but none that seem even vaguely appropriate. So he shoots from the hip, running the tip of the letter opener against the tip of his index finger.

"You sure she is on her way?" he asks Cole, sounding nervous like he's been set up on a blind date, and he wasn't sure if the woman would show up.

"Yes, Trenton she'll be here. This is an opportunity for her, and us too if you ask me. I'm surprised nobody has spotted her yet. She really is something else..." Cole replies, confirming everything that Trenton already knows about the beautiful songstress.

"That she is my man...that she is..." Trenton says in his usual trying-to-sound-younger-than-he-really-is way.

Toni arrives at the record label shortly before 11 AM and is shown into the office by a receptionist. The receptionist throws a look into the room that suggests that she has seen both men naked and that she knows the look that they are both giving Toni now, a look that says that her singing talent isn't the only reason she is here. She offers Toni a drink, and after Toni declines she leaves the room, although it is obvious that she would rather have stayed, to hear what they were going to talk about.

Trenton has fucked almost everybody in the office. The few he hasn't are either married, involved or lesbian. The lesbians have always held a special fascination for him too, but now that Toni is here, looking demure and unattainable in jeans and a silver t-shirt that says that she put in great effort not to appear like she was trying too hard. All these fantasies seem to be blowing somewhere on the outside of the thirteenth story with the winds akin to their altitude. Trenton and Cole are also good, not wanting any refreshments, ready to get on with the business of signing Toni. When the door closes, though, there is a very conspicuous silence in the room for a good minute.

Cole offers Toni a seat, and as she sits, Trenton looks away, out of the window. He seems to have a lot on his mind so that Toni wants to ask if she should perhaps come back later. But then Cole starts with the business at hand, going through the offer, outlining details of the contract that is duplicated in triplicate, a copy for each of them in the room. Toni reads the contract line for line, trying to make sense of the legal jargon while trying to listen to what Cole is saying at the same time. This is no easy fete.

Trenton says nothing throughout, just looking at Toni, more and more closely, but only when she is not looking at him. He really finds himself drawn to her, unnaturally it seems. There is nothing that can stop him from stealing glimpses of her, practically devouring her with his eyes. She feels this too, as she notices Trenton's eyes on her more and more. Toni doesn't give away the fact that she has seen him staring, though, trying to focus on her contract in front of her, and also trying to listen to Cole, who is still speaking, although a lot slower now.

What she hasn't noticed is Cole looking at her too. Both these men have undressed her over and over with their eyes, in their minds, their mouths salivating somewhat at the corners. Cole manages to compose himself enough to get through the contract, though, and then he asks Toni if there is anything that she doesn't understand. She offers up that perhaps she should take it away with her, and that she should probably get an attorney to look at it. Toni isn't sure if she said an attorney or her attorney, but it is too late for her to take it back now.

She gets up and finally looks at Trenton directly. She finds it strange that he hasn't said anything at all at this meeting. Toni raises her hand at him, and he takes it, running his fingers over hers tenderly before she pulls her hand away. She cannot make up her mind about Trenton, and she suddenly feels the need to leave. Cole walks her out of the office, passed the reception and into the elevator. As the doors close she tilts her head forward and then exhales hard as the doors close completely.

The atmosphere when Toni has finally cleared the building is very much more relaxed, Trenton suddenly having a lot to say to Cole, the proverbial cat seeming to have let go of his tongue at last.

"She is beautiful isn't she…" he says, stating the very obvious.

"Yes, that she is… and she's got a voice too, which is a good thing…That is why she was called in here today right, for her voice…" Cole just has to ask.

"Of course…yes… what other reason could there be…" Trenton answers, not really believing himself too much anymore.

It took three weeks for Cole to get Toni to believe that Live might sign her. And it took all of twenty minutes to go through the contract that, once signed, would mean that she belonged to them, artistically. Now the wait was on, for Toni to get back to them with the signed contract. If there was a problem with the contract, that would be a serious delay for Live. Cole goes over it alone in his office, making sure that if Toni did, in fact, solicit legal advice, that there was nothing untoward about the ten-page document. Two weeks go by before Toni calls Cole, ready to sign.

They meet at Live's offices again, Toni with a lawyer friend of a friends, just to be safe and come across as professional. The contract is fairly standard, though, and she has no arguments against it. She will have a full creative license, and Live will handle the business side of the arrangement. It is also only a two album deal, so if she doesn't feel the need to work with them after two albums, or if she doesn't produce significant enough returns for them, then the arrangement is terminated. Yes, it really was pretty standard.

The four of them, Toni, her lawyer, Cole, and Trenton meet in the boardroom at the opposite end of the hall where Trenton's office is located. The meeting goes well, and Trenton is a little chattier now, now that he knows that Toni is signing on the dotted line. He watches her fingers around the pen, and his thoughts go to his cock again. Imagining her fingers wrapped around his cock he starts to harden. But it is not just because of the thought of what could be a very elaborate hand job. Trenton really has the incredible urge to talk with Toni, alone. As the meeting comes to an end, he wonders what excuse he could use to get her on her own.

"Toni..." he says, as they get up to leave the room.

"Yes?" she asks.

"A moment, please..." he asks, trying to sound more relaxed than he actually is.

"Sure," she says, not sure at all what he could have to say to her that wasn't said in the meeting.

"I'm having a party, to celebrate...uhm...your signing, at my house, on Saturday...Be there..." he sounds like he is ordering her, but not. This confuses her a little, but since she is now finally in the big leagues, she knows that parties are going to become a way of life for her. And this party is especially for her, so of course, she will be there.

"Yes, of course, I'll be there. Thank you again for everything. And thank you for the freedom you have given me in the contract. I really didn't expect that..." she is babbling, and she doesn't know why. She is suddenly alone with Trenton, for the first time, and having all his attention is a little intimidating. She really wants to get out of here.

"Well, I find that the more freedom you give an artist, the better the final product is. You're going to be great...I predict that you are going to be exceptionally great indeed..." His tone is filled with innuendos, and Toni tries in vain to ignore them. But she is also intrigued by them, and she starts to think of Trenton in a way that their contractual relationship should really forbid.

Toni leaves the boardroom and meets Cole and Luke, her lawyer, at the elevator. After saying goodbye to Cole her and Luke get into the elevator and make their way out of the building. Luke is happy, and Toni is too, although she is not yet showing it. She will save her screaming and jumping up and down for the privacy of her apartment, which really won't be her apartment for much longer. She knows that her life is about to change, but just how much it will change is something that she cannot even comprehend. She is not prepared at all for the wild ride that is sure to follow.

Saturday is here sooner than she

thinks than she expects. Also, the signing bonus that she received is yet to clear in her struggling bank account, so she must rely on her old faithful items of clothing to make her first impression as a star. She takes out all of her dresses, all six of them, and lays them out on the bed. She immediately removes the cream number she wore to the audition, knowing that this would be a dead giveaway of her rather limited wardrobe. She is drawn to a dark gray mini-dress, not quite summer, but the most appropriate item if she thinks to make herself seen. And she really wants to be seen.

Toni knows that her real skill will be in her makeup. She knows just how to work with her complexion and the contours of her face. After showering and moisturizing, and getting dressed, she goes to work on her face. It takes twenty minutes, and when she is done, she looks at herself from various angles. She has got it just right. The pit of her stomach is like a boiling lava pit, though, and she isn't sure if she is ready to do this. She has to be, though.

She takes a cab to Trenton's house,

knowing that her car will not meet the requirements of her new life. Things are really about to change for her, and so she makes sure that she is ready for this change. Tonight is going to be the first insight into her new life, and she is as ready for it as she is going to be. The cab pulls up to the house, and Toni hands the cab driver almost all the money in her purse, except for ten dollars, the last note between her and her emergency fund.

The valet that comes up and opens the door for her is the same one that gave her the side eyes the last time she handed him the keys to her Honda, but he suddenly looks at her with a different eye. Everybody must have been told who the star is tonight, and she starts to feel every bit like a celebrity. Doors are opened for her, she is ushered into the main living area that leads to the terrace, and as soon as Cole sees her, he comes up to her and takes her away from the waiter who led her into the space.

Cole leads her to Trenton, who comes in and kisses the side of her face, breathing in the shampoo smell coming off her hair. It smells of apples, and he thinks cinnamon, but he isn't sure. He lingers on her neck, almost like a vampire, wanting to take a bite, but just in time, he pulls away from her. He looks at her in her eyes now and holds a glass of champagne up to her, which she takes from him and sips on it very slowly. Trenton removes her from Cole and starts to introduce her to a couple of important people in the room. By the time they have worked the room completely, Toni has finished her champagne.

Trenton pulls two glasses from a tray passing by them and then offers to show Toni the rest of his house. He doesn't even know what he is going to say to her when he finally gets her alone, but what he does know is that he needs to move her away from the crowd and see if he still feels the same way. As they get upstairs, Trenton showing her every room that they pass, before getting to his bedroom. Rather shyly, he walks her through the doors to the massive space, and she nervously follows him. The lights are off in the room, and Toni is suddenly very anxious.

But just as her eyes are processing

the darkness, there is light. Trenton watches as the lights in the space come on in waves, revealing parts of the room in succession. He loves this most about his bedroom, and he is suddenly very glad for this later addition to his bedroom because Toni looks impressed. Suddenly the fact that they are alone in the space settles on both of them, and they are both very anxious. Trenton has also closed the door to his bedroom, presumption overriding his common sense for a minute. He really doesn't know what to say to her.

Toni's heart starts to beat really fast, and she feels her hands sweating. She takes a sip from her glass, a small sip because she doesn't want to be finished with it. There is a strange comfort that she is finding in the glass, an escape into it from the glaring gaze of Trenton. He seems to want to say something to her, something that he is unable to articulate. She thinks she knows what it is, and she thinks that perhaps he could have waited for the ink to dry on her contract.

She wonders if this is the only reason she was signed, but then again, there would be easier ways for him to get her. She hasn't ever been with a white guy before, and she hasn't even thought of it. There are types of men, a sort of hierarchy in her head, but white guys feature somewhere between 'hell no' and 'it will never happen.' Now, though, it seems that it is going to happen, and she really doesn't feel that she is ready for this. Could her voice be her trump card, though, could it be enough of a trump for her to say no to Trenton?

She thinks though that she might not say yes, might not say no. There is something about Trenton that she finds unattractive, something about his bad boy persona that comes across in the way he speaks, even the way he walks. But something inside her, something in place of her that curiosity dwells, wants to know what he is capable of in bed. He hasn't made a move, though, and she wouldn't dream of it. There is a fine line between wanting a man and throwing yourself at one.

Trenton looks across the room for a bottle of champagne, and he finds one in an ice bucket in the corner. He always has his room prepared this way whenever he has parties. This is not the moment that he expected to crack open the bottle either, but their glasses are empty. He opens it and fills their glasses, Toni feeling like she should say something to him, but she just doesn't know what. She just holds her glass up to his and brings them together. Then she says thank you to him for taking the chance on her, and her music.

"You are a rare talent...we would be stupid to pass up an opportunity like this. You really are something special..." he says, looking her in her eyes, and saying more with them than he can bring himself with his mouth.

"Thank you Mr. Lively..." she says, wanting to come across as professional as possible, given the situation, given the place where they now find themselves.

"Trenton, please...call me Trenton..." he says, as he sips on his glass and then refills it. They look at one another again, for the longest time. The silence is remarkably awkward, and so they laugh at themselves and each other in the end. They look away from each other, and then back to one another. The tension seems to lift in the room suddenly, and Trenton is really taken aback by her beautiful smile.

He walks to the terrace doors and opens them up. He calls her to him, and they walk out onto the balcony together. They both look down at the party that is really developing now, but with a subtle sophistication that Toni cannot help but think is just for her. She likes it, and she enjoys the feeling on the balcony, the feeling of being on top of the world. She cannot wait to move out of the apartment that she is currently living at, wanting to be gone out of there tonight, right now. But she knows that she will have to wait until the check clears.

Trenton waves at someone who has just arrived at the party, and who happens to look up just in time to see him standing on his balcony. The actress waves back and Toni is suddenly filled with the feeling of being taken and placed on cloud nine and promised to be kept there for as long as she wants to. The actress waves at Toni too, and she lifts her hand casually, even though her stomach is turning and her heart is threatening to beat out of her chest. She really is feeling like she is in the inner circle now, and this is a place that she can enjoy being in.

She feels Trenton's eyes on her again. She doesn't look at him, though, wondering what it is that he is playing at, or what he really wants from her. If it was just sex, then surely he would have made his move by now. But he just seems to watch her, observe her every movement. Toni starts to feel a little uncomfortable, but she hides it exceptionally well. There is nothing that she can do if he does make a move too, except to say no and move on away from him. Surely he cannot tear up her contract, now that it is signed, and signed in the presence of a witness who had nothing to do with Live Records.

Her curiosity is getting to her, though, and the feeling moves into her belly, and down between her legs. She crosses them over each other and raises her eyes to meet Trenton's for the first time in what feels like forever. He is really staring at her now and moving closer to her. Her heart is really beating now, really going crazy in her chest. Toni can only hope that he doesn't see how nervous she is.

He moves her hair out of her eyes, something that she was actually hoping to achieve with the home-treatment relaxer she used just that afternoon. She really cannot wait until she can afford to go to a professional salon and really get herself treated. Manicures and pedicures are on the top of her list, and a professional relax. A facial and full body massage will also be nice, as soon as her check clears. She felt butterflies, real butterflies when she called the bank to confirm that the check had actually been deposited.

Of course, it was because she deposited it herself. It is really a liberating feeling. She looks at Trenton again, closely now, and she sees him for the first time. His eyes are a beautiful green, and his face has just enough stubble on it to look rough. His top two buttons are undone on his shirt too so that she sees that he has a very hairy chest. Her eyes fall on his crotch, and she quickly moves them away, not sure why she looked down there. He has noticed this, though, and he smiles to himself.

They are both checking each other out, both undressing one another, and this makes them both more comfortable. At least the interest isn't one sided, but the situation is more than a little inconvenient. Trenton is the owner of the label that has just signed Toni, and she is for all intents and purposes an up and coming black songstress. The combination would get more than a few people talking. Trenton isn't even sure if he wants a relationship with her, or if he just wants to fuck her, but one thing is certain, he really wants her.

Toni isn't sure too of what this situation could be. If she lets him take her, and they have sex, then the line would be crossed, and she might not be able to concentrate on fulfilling her end of the contract. She starts to think that maybe she should get out of here and that maybe she should suggest that they get back to the party. But Trenton is coming closer to her still, and she cannot move out of the way. Oh god, what is going to happen here now, and how will she respond.

Trenton leans over to her and takes the side of her face in his hand. He pulls her head up to his and kisses her cheek. Then he kisses her ear, and whispers into it, softly. "Welcome to my world..." he says, and then kisses her again on her ear, and on her cheeks. He pulls her face away a little and then starts to go for her mouth. When he lands on her lips, she drops her glass. As it shatters on the floor, he doesn't even skip a beat, kissing her lips tenderly without using his tongue at all, just touching his lips to hers over and over again.

Toni thinks of what he has just said to her. Welcome to my world, he said. Just what world is that? What does he mean by it? Is it his world up here away from everyone else, or is it the whole of everything, the craziness of the ride that is about to come? She doesn't know, and this not knowing settles over her with a resigned acceptance. What she does know now, more than she did before they walked into Trenton's bedroom, that whatever world he is talking about, she is about to find out...

6

The weeks following the signing are really a rollercoaster. There are many ups, and a couple of downs, but the downs are so few, and far between that, they are mostly negligible. The ups, though are magnificent. Just how quickly her life changed is even beyond her, far beyond all her expectations. She tries to hold back too, but Toni knows that the sooner she embraces all these changes, the sooner she can focus on the real change, the opportunity to make music professionally.

As soon as her check cleared, she moved out of her apartment. She forfeited her deposit because she moved out without serving her full notice, unable to stop herself from moving into the upmarket penthouse near downtown Los Angeles. The reason she chose this particular apartment is because firstly, she really liked it, and secondly because it was five minutes ride from the Live Records recording studios. She knows that she wants to move closer to the beach, but that will come later when she purchases her first home. For now, she is renting, and so this penthouse is, in a word, perfect.

The place is unfurnished, and it takes just a weekend to kit it out. Toni never really thought too much about personal taste, not until now, not until she could afford to have personal taste. Looking around the space, though, she realizes that she is very minimalist. The colors too are very neutral, grays, blacks, and whites, with splashes of red. As she takes in the sunset on her large, red leather sofa in her living room, sipping champagne alone, she lets out a sigh, knowing that at last, she has arrived. Tomorrow is her first day in the studio, but there are no expectations of her, just a jamming session with a producer.

She walks into the studio, with shorts, a tank, slip slops and her guitar. Not that she doesn't feel the need to put in any effort because she has. The shorts are stylish denim, with metal press studs, and the tank is a mixture of grays, the understated kind of expensive that lets you know, without screaming it, that it cost more money than she has spent on food in a whole month, before this exciting time in her life. The thongs on her feet are slivers of black, too expensive for what they are, but where she shops now have changed, dramatically.

Toni doesn't even have a purse on her, just her keys tucked into the pocket of her jean shorts. She walked the few blocks to the studio, guitar over her shoulder, feeling very bohemian, very New York. But this isn't New York, and thankfully so. LA weather makes her outfit more than a little appropriate. In the studio, she tries not to be in awe of the stars that have come through these very walls. She looks at the producer sitting casually in jeans and a t-shirt, watches her set herself up on the couch.

"Toni, Toni, Toni..." the producer says after he has introduced himself as CJ, and she doesn't know if she should laugh at his reference to the 90s RnB group.

"Do I just play?" she asks, never really working with anyone before in her process, but she knows that they aren't trying to achieve anything today. It really just is about them getting to know each other. They vibe well enough too, and after two hours they have some really good material. There is nothing solid, though, but everything has been recorded, so they have something to reference later. For now, though, thoughts turn to lunch.

"Should we order something up, or do you wanna maybe get out of her for a bit?" CJ asks, his eyes unable to peel away from her thighs. Those shorts really are short, and her thighs are really very distracting. He reminds himself to be professional. The artist is usually the one who falls for the producer, and so he just has to wait for her to lust after him.

"We could order in, I think that we're getting some really good material. I want to keep working. Can I have a chicken wrap?" she asks, really needing the delicious comfort of chicken right now, for no reason other than the familiarity of it. She loves chicken, loved it in her former life, and she really loves it now. There are some things that don't deserve to die a lonely death on the road to stardom. Grilled chicken in a wrap is one of those things. CJ laughs at her, not knowing if she is serious or not. She is, and so he gets a runner to pick up their lunch.

Trenton brings the lunch into the studio, something which catches both Toni and CJ by complete surprise. They both had no idea that Trenton would even be in the building today. Not that they would know, mind you since his PA hardly ever knew where he was or what he would be doing. And to have him in the studio is a rare treat, CJ not able to remember a single time since he started working at Live ever seeing Trenton in the studio. But here he was, and he was carrying their lunch.

"So, who's going to share with the delivery guy?" Trenton asks a look so serious on his face that they are both not sure if he is joking or not. He must be, right? Toni is the first to venture a laugh, followed tentatively by CJ. Trenton squints, looking from one to the other, holding up the chicken wrap in one hand and the Chinese in the other, like he was asking them whose was whose. CJ is the first to answer this time, taking the packets from Trenton, laying the food out buffet-style, except for my wrap, which he hands to me.

Trenton really does share CJs meal, leaving her to her meal. They speak mostly to each other, about Toni, strangely enough, as if she wasn't even there. She puts this off to the way things worked in the real music world, and she just sits in the corner, eating her wrap, listening to the riffs and chords that they had put together that morning. Trenton is listening too, but pretending not to. He is also pretending not to be looking at Toni, which he is, and she is pretending not to notice.

His eyes linger over her legs, long toned chocolate legs that end too soon it seems, in shorts. Trenton really wishes that the shorts were suddenly gone. CJ has wished the same thing all morning, but he is relying on his game. Both men's eyes fall all over Toni now, resting too long over her breasts, and when she looks up, they linger still, before they look away. Then Trenton starts a conversation with CJ again, including Toni this time, but the conversation really isn't going anywhere, because there was no initial direction for it to begin with. Toni is clever, though, and she just goes with it.

The conversation flows easier now, so easy that they find themselves talking way past lunch. But there really is no timeline, and today isn't really a formal day's work. Nothing is formal it seems, and Toni really likes this. She likes the fact that CJ is easy to talk to, and that he really just lets he be free, with her music. Trenton morphs from super-talkative to deadly silent, and this throws Toni a little. She really has no idea that Trenton has never been involved with any artist, not until now. So she just puts it down to the way he is.

This really isn't how he is, though.

He is drawn to Toni, really drawn. He doesn't know though if it is just because he wants to fuck her, or if he wants to get to know her. There is just something so alluring about Toni, something that Trenton wants to have, to own. The idea of ownership is one that is very warped in his head, though, always, always getting what he wants. He is unsure though of what exactly it is that he really wants from Toni. And now, watching her in her element, CJ working the technology while she works with just her voice and guitar, this uncertainty grows exponentially.

He knows too that he should probably leave, but it is almost six PM, and he starts to think that maybe, just maybe he should ask Toni to dinner. Maybe he should ask both of them to dinner, just so that he has someone to break the ice. He doesn't know how easy the conversation would flow if it were just him and Toni there. Perhaps he should call Cole, and make it a group thing. Shit, his head is really spinning now.

At 8 he is still there, just hanging around. CJ and Toni start to wrap things up, though, so he knows it is now or never. He thinks again of calling Cole, but looking at the time, he thinks that maybe he will be pulling him from a meeting. They really do work well for him, and they work really hard. He knows this, even though he doesn't really say it to them very often. Eventually, he breathes in, and holding his breath, he just lets the words fall from his lips. "Dinner?"

"Sure?" CJ answers, looking at Toni, who seems to be on his team now. They really gelled very well today, and so together, they feel like they can humor the boss, for a few hours.

"As long as it is somewhere that will work with my outfit..." Toni says, laughing, but serious at the same time.

"I know just the place..." Trenton says as he holds the door open for Toni and CJ. They leave the building and walk towards the parking. Trenton came on his bike, so he says that CJ and Toni must just follow him. They make their way in convoy to a cute Mexican place on Sunset.

The casual Trio walks into jalapeño shortly before 9. Trenton orders champagne, just one bottle, though, and raises his glass to Toni. CJ raises his glass too, and then the three glasses come together and then find their individual mouths. They order and settle into a casual conversation about the music business, and being in it at this point in history. CJ does most of the talking, though, Trenton is careful not to give away that he just really fell into the business, with no solid foundation in anything music. He makes a mental note to learn as much about the industry that facilitates his lifestyle as he can in the next couple of days if just to impress Toni.

The conversation moves easily on from music quickly enough, though, and they really just start talking about everything that would get them to know each other. Trenton and Toni are both more and more intrigued with each other, not that any of them is showing it, though. They just laugh cautiously at each other's jokes, using CJ as the human buffer they need to get into each other, scratching a little more below the surface. There are so many levels it seems, to Trenton, and Toni finds herself more and more curious. She pulls herself back from the edge just in time, though, just before she gives away more of herself than she intends to.

It is almost 1 AM when the three of them finally leave the restaurant slash pub. Trenton says goodbye rather quickly, needing to be away from Toni now, not liking the feelings that are developing inside him rather quickly for the beautiful young woman. He wonders what it is about her that has him in a real bind, what witchcraft she has used on him to get him so intrigued. He needs to be away from her, but every part of him just wants to be with her, in her, all over her. This confusion drives him insane, and the air hitting his face on the ride home does nothing to free him from these thoughts that have tangled a serious web over him, in his head, and dare he says, his heart.

Toni is also quiet in the car. CJ tries to talk to her, but after a while he gives up, knowing that she has something else on her mind. He manages to get her address from her, though, and they drive in silence to her apartment building. CJ half hopes that she will invite him in, for a nightcap, for more maybe, but she obviously has another man on her mind. Damn Trenton, playing the game that he already thought he had a handle on. Damn him.

She does kiss him goodbye, though, on his cheek, and then the other one. She makes it all the way to her apartment without even thinking, as though she has lived here forever. Her mind is flooded with thoughts of the music mogul who made an impromptu appearance at her studio session today, the man who brought their lunch into the studio, and then took them out for dinner. She will not allow herself to think that this means anything more than it does, but secretly, in that place where no one can see, she hopes it does.

In the shower, she thinks of Trenton still, wondering if he too is thinking of her. How can someone have such a monumental effect on you within such a short space of time? How can she even be thinking the thoughts that are running through her head, like flash images on a TV screen? She really doesn't know, but what she knows is that she wants to know more about him. She wants to scratch more that beneath the surface, and get to the nuts and bolts of this man that seemed to her so unattainable just a few days ago. Now she dares believe that something has started here.

There is, however, the possibility that it is all in her mind, that she is seeing things that aren't there. But she has always had a sense for these things, always been able to read between the many lines that are often drawn across flirtations and other forms of human interaction. This is a whole other ballgame, though, she knows this. This man, in fact, every man that she met because of signing with Live is a completely different beast. They are still men, but they really do operate on a whole other value system, one where the lines of morality are extremely jaded.

She thinks about these differences, adjusting the heat in the shower by turning the hot water a little higher. Toni had always found men to be remarkably simple beings. Until she met Cole, and Trenton, and even CJ. They seem to have agendas to their agendas, and this makes them difficult to read. She has known some of them longer than others, but it is the same with each of them. There is something about this new breed of man that she finds remarkably complicated.

Is it not this complication that has her now drawn to Trenton, she wonders. Does she just want to prove to herself that she can have any man that she wants? Hardly, she thinks, never quite being that girl. There is just something about him that has sparked a curiosity in her, she admits, and this is something that she will explore given half the chance. But when will she have the chance to really explore this newfound curiosity? She puts her head under the shower spray now and tries to wash these thoughts down the drain with the water now falling directly on her head.

She washes herself free from these thoughts and walks out of the bathroom with a towel wrapped tightly around her. She goes to the kitchen and pours herself a glass of wine, taking it with her to the rooftop terrace, a space that is all hers, one of the perks of having the penthouse apartment. She sips slowly, taking in the air, crisp, fresh, remarkably warm, and throws her eyes over the city that will spring to life in just a few hours. She puts off tonight as a random night of fun, resolving not to think about it again, not to think about Trenton again. She knows though that this will be far more easily said than done.

Near the coast, in Malibu, Trenton is sipping on a vodka and cranberry juice, on his own terrace. He knows what he wants to be thinking about, who he wants to be thinking about, but he deliberately moves his mind from Toni. He thinks, for the first time in a long time, about his business, the inheritance that he got too soon, and of all the things that he should know by now but doesn't. He thinks about the various levels of the music industry, and how he should, in fact, have a handle on all these levels.

The one thing that he knows he should probably have had a handle on by now is spotting talent. People are relying on him to have an ear for newcomers, or at least they should. But he knows that they don't, just passing ideas by him, people that they have already decided on but just as a courtesy ask for his opinion. He has agreed with every selection made by his team over the last few years, and they have all paid off. But he has never had an opinion that was really worth anything.

He hates that he has just been a figurehead really, just an ornament. Owning Live Records in name only, he has just been coasting it really. How does one develop an ear for this sort of thing, though, he wonders? How does one develop this muscle, and how does one grow it? Is it something that can be developed in fact, or is it just the luck of the draw, you either being born with it or not? This is something that really bothers him suddenly.

Again though he finds his mind going to Toni. Her voice really is something special, and he isn't the one who found her. He wouldn't have even met her or heard her if it wasn't for Cole. He makes a mental note to start going to the little places that up and coming talent performs at, where these gems, these diamonds in the rough can be found. There is something that still nags at him, though, through all his attempts at thinking shop. He really is very attracted to Toni, and this attraction has nothing to do with her voice.

He pours himself another drink, and looks through his phone, checking his booty calls, knowing that even though it is late, or early, depending on how you look at it, any one of them will come flying to him, ready to satisfy him, and themselves. There is something about the power that he has that has jaded him, almost completely, and this power really has corrupted him absolutely. He looks at the pictures attached to the contact information, and notices, not surprisingly, that none of them are black. He thinks of the escorts that he had, the tag team of the Russian and the Black girl, and he remembers the sweetness of both their pussies. Why did he have to pay for a black woman to fuck him?

Randomly, he calls a girl, called Tania, and he knows that she is still sleeping by the sound of her voice, but that she is trying to sound more alert than he knows she is. He doesn't know even when the last time was that she was with him, but that doesn't matter because she says that she will be here in an hour, and he is happy. At least this will offer him a distraction from Toni, which is something that he really needs now. He knows, in that part of him that cares about his business that Toni is different, and that fucking her and leaving her could jeopardize Cole's investment in her.

It is actually his investment, but he knows how this game has worked up until now. He makes up his mind to be more hands on it his business, as he finishes his drink and jumps in the shower, pulling on his cock, just to empty it before Tania arrives, wanting to have a long, languid session of fucking with her. He wants to fuck her until the sun comes up, something which is more than possible now that he has squirted his first load in the shower, and it is almost 3:30 AM. She arrives on cue, and he lets her into his house, offering her a drink, which she accepts before following him upstairs to his bedroom.

Trento really enjoys Tania too, although he really cannot remember her from the last time they were together. He must have been seriously wired, and very drunk. But now she is here, and she is keen to do a few lines, which is the first thing that he likes about her. There is nothing worse than being with a stuck up woman who doesn't do drugs, and worse, who has a problem with him doing drugs. So they do a few lines together, and then get naked. She is very good at sucking cock too, which he absolutely loves. She knows just how he likes to be sucked.

The sun comes up, and Trenton is still inside her. He really is going at her with all his power, and he really has a lot of it. By midday they have done more lines than are practical, feeling like they could go on all day. They have also had several orgasms, and Trenton is very satisfied. Tania too is happy, but she suddenly needs to go. Trenton isn't against her leaving, strangely enough, and after seeing her out he throws himself in his swimming pool, feeling like he hasn't lost himself, at least. He will call another girl later, but he finds himself thinking, as he does a few laps of the pool, about what Toni might be doing at the studio with CJ. CJ is very attractive, and he is black, and suddenly Trenton is very nervous. He feels that if he loses Toni to a producer, somebody will have to be fired.

7

Two days later he cannot hold himself back, making his way to the studio just before 10. He isn't even sure if Toni will be there, and he doesn't think to call ahead. He just needs to see her, wants to see her. He walks into the studio and finds her and CJ already hard at work, pulling together a song, a real song, seemingly out of nowhere. It is absolutely beautiful to watch.

Trenton holds a coffee cup in one hand, a Frappuccino from the place around the corner, and when he sees that they are here, he thinks that maybe he should have brought them coffee too. But he looks around the studio and notices that there are two coffee cups and some Danish on the table, so he feels like he dodged a bullet on that one. He greets them after they finish the phrase they are working on, and Toni just nods in his direction. There is something similar to tension in the room suddenly, but since nobody can put their finger on it, nobody says anything.

He watches them as they continue the work, finishing up the song, and then high fiving each other, half hugging, and then laughing out loud at their achievement. They return to the part of the studio, on the other side of the glass, the part where Trenton is sitting on the couch sipping on his coffee, and they greet him again. There is something even thicker in the air now that they are breathing the same air, in the same space. Trenton watches CJ and Toni closely, looking for anything that will give away anything over and above the professional relationship between artist and producer.

CJ and Trenton talk for a moment, and then CJ leaves the room, needing the bathroom suddenly. Trenton is suddenly very nervous alone with Toni, and he hates that he is suddenly out of his depth, out of his comfort zone. What is it about her that makes him so uncomfortable? Whatever it is, he cannot shake it, and with Toni coming close to him now, too close, leaning over him to get her coffee, taking it to her mouth, watching him over the rim of the takeaway coffee cup.

Trenton too is watching her, their eyes finding and losing each other as they try not to look like they are actually staring at each other, although that is exactly what they are doing. Suddenly they both go very quiet, and then, after a moment, they both burst out laughing. The tension is really so thick in the room that they cannot help but laugh. This relieves the mood somewhat, but they still don't have nothing to talk about. At least they cannot think of what to say to each other at the moment, so they laugh again and then look away.

Toni really wants CJ to come back into the studio, but he must have got distracted by something, or someone, on the outside. She searches her head for something to say, anything that will break this deadlock, but nothing comes to mind, adding to her anxiety.

Trenton looks at her again, really looks at her, and she has no choice but to just let him. At least she looks more and more like she belongs in this world, this world that seemed so far away just a few weeks ago. Now, though, she really has her look on lockdown.

There is something that feels more comfortable too with this new look. She is wearing jeans, off-cut and ripped. They look very expensive yet not. They are of course. She is wearing a t-shirt, tight, form-fitting, with a picture of the statue of liberty down the front. She looks like she wouldn't be lost in New York, but just as comfortable in LA, and she feels very comfortable too. Her feet are bare because her sandals are next to her bag. They wouldn't even cover her feet if she were wearing them, though, so she doesn't feel too exposed.

She also has very pretty toes, so that she really is happy that he can see them. Toni wonders why she really wants Trenton to approve of her, but she does. And he seems to approve too because he cannot take his eyes off her. She sips on her empty coffee cup now, knowing that she needs a crutch, but not having anything else to turn to. Eventually, she tosses the cup in the bin, not sure why, but needing to do something with herself. Then she turns to Trenton, and finally thinks of something to say.

"So, do you like what you hear so far?" she asks him, thinking that the best thing to do is to keep the conversation on things that are relevant and current.

"Definitely...Yeah... I can't wait until you bust out your first CD or a single at least... And by the look of things, that won't be very long from now..." Trenton says, responding to her question in much more detail that was really required.

"No pressure..." she says, with a smile on her face.

"Yeah definitely...No pressure..." Trenton responds, meaning it.

CJ returns just in time to break the awkward silence as soon as it returns. Toni is relieved, as is Trenton so that they both turn to CJ and start chatting with him at the same time. He notices that they are both somewhat uncomfortable, so he takes the conversation on a new trip, and they seem to ease up a little bit. He suddenly feels like a referee, hating this middle man situation that he finds himself in. There are ways to get out of it, though, but none that come to mind immediately. He just keeps the conversation flowing, and then suggests that they get back to work.

Toni loses herself in her music now, really loses herself. She goes to that place inside herself where nothing else matters, where it's just her and her guitar, making love to each other, dancing a strange reciprocal tango and then leaving each other just out of reach. There is nothing else in the room now, no Trenton, no CJ, nothing. There are no computers or sound equipment. There is just Toni and the song in her heart. It is beautiful. It is also this way for a good couple of hours so that lunch is again ordered in, and they work well until after 10 that night.

Trenton was perhaps right. Maybe it would be sooner rather than later that she released her first studio album. He is also still here, even after he should have long left the studio. CJ and Toni wrap up the day, happy with what they have done for the day, feeling strangely satisfied, fulfilled even. Trenton says nothing as they finish up, talking mostly to each other. He just watches them, enjoying the view of Toni even more now, now that she is getting ready to leave, now that she seems suddenly available for him to take her out alone.

When CJ and Toni leave the studio, Trenton in tow, Trenton wants to ask Toni to dinner, without CJ, he questions himself suddenly. He starts to doubt himself, worried that he might have nothing to say to her once he gets her alone. If, as is a distinct possibility, the attraction is just a sexual one, and he just wants to fuck her, then there really will be no need for conversation. If this is the case, though, then how would he ask Toni the burning question, addressing the elephant in the room?

"Do you want to grab a bite to eat?" he asks her, as he holds the door open for her and CJ. She looks at CJ, who seems to know that the invitation isn't extended to him as well, because he just says good night to them, and walks to his own car. Toni is left alone with Trenton, not sure what she should say, knowing what she wants to say but shouldn't. She says it anyway.

"Uhm...sure...did you come with your car today?" I ask him, trying to lighten the mood, remembering that he came with his bike the last time.

"Yes...this way..." he says, and walks her to his Aston Martin. Her guitar just about fits in the boot, but she is really not happy being separated from her instrument this way. There is something almost animate about her guitar, and she suffers from serious separation anxiety when it is out of her reach for too long. She breathes, though, counting slowly back from ten in her head so that she can make her peace with the fact that the guitar is stuck in the boot of a car, like a body in a trunk, ready for burial.

We drive through to a place on Rodeo, which is really nicer than any restaurant than she has ever been in. She feels strangely underdressed for this trendy spot, though, and she wishes that she had gone home to dress first. Too late now, though, and they make their way to the table near the back, near the large windows that look into a center courtyard, and are seated in a relaxed booth, ordering drinks. The tension returns briefly, but then Toni decides that they are just being silly, and since there are no expectations on any of them from each other, she thinks, there really is no need for them to be awkward with one another.

When their drinks arrive, it is Toni who addresses the seeming elephant in the room, at least one of them. She does this quickly, catching Trenton by surprise. "So, why am I here?" she asks him, casually. This question is anything but casual, though, at least not for her. She really wants to know what Trenton wants from her before she lets her imagination run away with her and she starts to see and believe things that really aren't there at all.

"I thought that would be obvious..." Trenton says, mimicking her casualness.

"Let's pretend that it's not..." she says, pressing him for an answer.

Trenton looks at her and squints. He raises and lowers just one eyebrow, looking at her closely, searching his head for a response rather quickly. She is also looking at him closely now, too closely, so that he knows that everything hangs on the words that are about to come out of his mouth. He thinks carefully, very carefully about what he is going to say, the pressure of it all hitting him hard in his chest now, like a ten-ton truck.

"Well, to be honest, I don't know. I really find you quite intriguing, and I guess I just want to get to know you a little better...that's all..." Trenton says, not sure how he has come across. He knows just that he has been honest, perhaps too honest, but that it is too late for him to take back what he has just said. The words have come out of his mouth, and they have fallen on the ears of the woman sitting across him in the comfortable booth. He braces himself for her response.

Toni smiles, not really knowing what to say. She hadn't expected this, but it is very nice to hear. She doesn't even respond to his statement at all, just moving the conversation on from there, but keeping the way his words made her feel close to the surface. They really were unexpected proclamations, and she isn't even sure of an appropriate response. So she doesn't respond to it exactly, keeping the conversation light and easy from that point on. There is something about keeping things easy that sort of lifts the veil on the people at the table, and they are suddenly free with each other.

They are free with each other several times over the next couple of weeks. When they are walking on the beach just a stone's throw away from Trenton's house, talking about the development of her up and coming album, which is coming together really quickly, Trenton looks at her hands, an ice-cream between her fingers. The details of her hands are suddenly crystal clear, almost as though she were really visible to him for the first time. He looks up at her face, her lips mostly, and they too are suddenly clear as daylight to him.

He really wants to kiss her now, more than anything in the world. They have been seeing each other for about three weeks now, although there is nothing set in stone, no confirmation either way of what they are to each other. They both suck the remainder of their ice-creams, left with nothing but sticks in their mouths. Trenton watches as she moves the stick between her lips, and then between her teeth. As she removes the stick from her mouth completely, his cock goes hard a little. He doesn't even realize it, only when he sees her eyes on his shorts does he know that he has a growing problem.

There is no way for him to hide it too, Toni's eyes on the growing cock too quickly. What she was doing looking at his crotch he doesn't know, but her eyes are still glued to his cock, which has firmed considerably now. He puts his hand over his cock, on the bulge, trying to hide himself from the woman that has already seen too much. His cock starts to give, thankfully, and it goes softer, making the hand over cock unnecessary. He takes his hands and cups her face, pulling her closer to him.

They have not kissed yet, and they have not come close to kissing before. There is something about this moment that seems to be the right time, the perfect moment for them to finally kiss. He pulls her closer, and he comes down to her, meeting her in midair until their lips are about to touch. His nose touches hers, and he pauses. Then suddenly he puts his mouth on hers, and her eyes close. He starts to kiss her, and she is frozen, for a moment, not sure how to respond to this situation.

Trenton keeps on kissing her, with just his lips, still trying to pull some sort of response from her. She warms to him at last, the shock fading, and the feeling of his lips on hers is finally responded to. They kiss each other now, still with just their lips, but at least they are working together. The kiss is long too, and very, very intense. Never before had Trenton believed that a kiss could be so passionate, so intense, and all without even releasing his tongue from his mouth once. Toni too is taken aback, this being the first time that she has kissed a white man.

She had never thought of it before, not until now, not until he actually started kissing her. There is no difference really in the way he kisses her too, accept the absence of tongue, which is becoming more and more conspicuous. She thinks of feeding him her tongue first but knows somehow that he needs to be in control of this situation in its totality. Toni doesn't mind giving him this control either, just letting it happen, enjoying it. And she really is enjoying it more and more with each moment that passes.

When Trenton finally sends his tongue into her mouth, she almost doesn't believe it. She takes it into her mouth, though, and moves her tongue over it, their tongues snaking around each other now, moving hard against one another. Then he pulls his tongue from her mouth and settles his lips on hers directly, sucking her mouth into his almost. Then he lets her mouth free, and he looks at her, in her eyes, to see if she approves. He really needs for her to have enjoyed this kiss, almost as much as he has.

She smiles at him, and then takes his face in her hands now, pulling him down to her again. Toni settles her lips on his again and sucks his mouth into hers now, and he knows that she really enjoyed it. She sends her tongue into his mouth immediately, not waiting as long as he did before he did the same. She really works her tongue on every part of his mouth, and he is the one who is taken aback now. She seems to have come out of her shell, more in the last minute than in the last three weeks, and he really likes this Toni.

They kiss for the longest time, and then they suddenly separate. Trenton kisses her on her forehead, and then on her cheeks. Then he kisses her on her nose, and laughs out loud, taking her nose between his lips and really enjoying the fact that she seems to be smiling more openly now. She really seems to enjoy his silliness. This is something that nobody ever gets to see because he is always on some power trip or acting a fool, drunk or wired or both. There is something really refreshing about this side of Trenton, and Toni plans to enjoy it.

He plays with her along the beach, as they walk the full length of it, the sand between their toes, on their feet. She relaxes more and more in his company, and by the time they are back at the house, the both of them are really acting more and more like a couple that has been dating for a very long time. The lunch prepared for them goes down well too, and they continue to enjoy each other's company for the rest of the afternoon. By the time Toni is dropped back at her house just before 6, and without Trenton being too presumptuous, he asks to be let up.

Toni knows that it is too soon for them to go to the next level, and so she lets him know in no uncertain terms that, while it has been good, she really needs to get some rest. She knows though that she will not sleep for a while yet because the excitement of the kiss still hangs heavy around her like the fruits on a tree. They kiss again, for a long time, and then Toni gets out of the car and goes into her building. She cannot wait to get into the safety of her apartment so that she can scream into a pillow.

As soon as she gets into her apartment, she doesn't go straight to the room, for her pillows. She goes instead straight for the roof terrace and looks out over the setting sun. She screams loudly, into the city, the excitement and joy uncontainable any longer. She really is happy, happier than she has been in a long, long time. Words cannot describe how she is feeling really, but she knows that it feels very good.

There are still thoughts, though, of Trenton, and his character. Thoughts of his reputation bother her a little bit, but she knows that she has seen a part of him that nobody really ever gets to see. Or is it that this is what he wants her to think? She is suddenly not sure, hating this uncertainty for everything that it represents. She thinks of her past relationships now and really doesn't know what it is about Trenton, other than his race that is, that makes him different from the other men she has dated. Toni is suddenly a little conflicted.

The rumors about Trenton really are everywhere. You cannot miss his escapades, they're in every tabloid. The back pages of every paper are riddled with pictures of the music industry bad boy, and whether or not you believe what you see and read, you are definitely drawn to the stories. There are many of them too, but they all follow a common thread, of sex, drugs, alcohol, and scorned women. This, in a nutshell, is everything that the public knows about Trenton. So Toni feels like he has let her into places that nobody else has seen.

The pictures of Trenton with different women are also all over the internet. Toni cannot help but google him now, pouring herself a glass of red, needing it to make the pictures a little easier to swallow. Much against her better judgment, and against her own inhibitions, she deliberately looks for pictures of Trenton with black girls. She needs to know if she is just a once off, or if she is just a novelty to tick off on his box of people to do. She thinks of the past few weeks with him and really cannot think that it is the case. Maybe, like her, he just hasn't had the opportunity to explore across the color line.

After another glass of red, and more perusing of the pages that come up in response to Trenton Lively, she is more confused than she was at the onset. She tries to take a fresh look at the information being fed up to her from her tablet, but there really is no sugarcoating anything that she sees. The headlines are clear. The pictures are clear, no hint or trace of Photoshop anywhere. So she knows that she must accept that it is the truth and that everything that she is seeing is exactly what it is.

Toni is a big girl, though, she knows this. She accepts that Trenton has a past and that he has a present. She accepts that she might just be passing through his life, and he through hers, but there is something about him that makes her want to save him from himself, almost. But this is not a very good foundation for a relationship, so she just resolves to get to know him a little better with the passage of time, over the next few weeks.

The next few weeks do go by without incident, and he seems to have stayed out of the public eye. The tabloids are even asking questions about where he is, and what has become of Trenton Lively. There is nothing in the papers about Toni and Trenton at all, and this doesn't bother her. But she does start to notice that they go to places where the chances of being stalked by the paparazzi are zero to none, and this really starts to bother her. Is he hiding her from public view? Surely not, she thinks.

Publicly there are appearances by Toni, introductions into the music industry, pegging her as the next big thing. She likes the attention too and focuses even harder on her single, and her whole album actually. There is something about being happy with someone that really gets her creative juices flowing. She churns out a new song almost every day now, and every day that she goes into the studio she comes out of it with a rough cut to a new track. Everything is going well for her, on every level, and she really thinks that there is nothing that could possibly make things any better.

The unspoken pressure for them to have sex starts to build, though. There is nothing blatant about it, nothing explicit, but there is just a tension building between them when they are alone, and this has everything to do with Trenton wanting to sleep with Toni, and Toni wanting to be slept with. This is very strange that two adults don't have the guts to say what they want, and also that, after such a long time of sort of dating, it is still unclear what they actually are to each other. Toni needs to know more than Trenton though, and she really starts to look for signs of what she is exactly to the music man.

8

About two months after they start seeing each other, Toni feels the pressure. There is nothing said specifically in line with 'shall we fuck,' but she feels like maybe it is time for her to put out. But she really wants it to be special, and since Trenton hasn't said anything about it, she puts it off to her own preconceptions. She could have it all wrong, or maybe she wants to sleep with him more than him her.

But Trenton also really wants to sleep with Toni. He isn't sure about why he has carried on with her for so long with no indication of getting into her panties, but he must admit that he really just enjoys her company. And the first kiss was beautiful, as have been the subsequent ones. He really loves being with her, but now he really wants to be inside her. He has never waited so long to be with a woman, like that, and this is starting to feel like a monumental series of firsts. There must be something in the air, he thinks.

Tonight they go to the beach and sit in the car eating Chinese. This is so student-like, and it would be cheap if they weren't in an Aston Martin, that both of them cannot hide their amusement. It was Trenton's idea, his take on that old classic drive-in date. And it wasn't altogether unpleasant, so they really just relax into enjoying each other's company. And they really do enjoy one another, so much that it is almost midnight when they realize that they have actually finished eating, and have spent more than the requisite time kissing.

Trenton is hard now, so hard that he feels like he is going to burst. He adjusts his cock in his pants, but it offers him absolutely no relief. He really doesn't know what to do about it, but he knows what he would like to do with his erection. There is just one thing on his mind now, and there is just one thing that will placate his raging cock. But how does he ask her, how does he even suggest that they go back to his place. Or maybe they could go back to her place. Actually, Trenton realizes, as he sends his tongue into Toni's mouth again, that he has yet to be invited up to her place.

When they get to her building, they kiss some more in the car. He really wants to be invited up, but he will not force her to invite him if she doesn't want to. He really starts to think that perhaps she doesn't want to, but then suddenly she says 'do you want to come up for a drink,' and this seals the deal. He starts to believe that tonight might be the night, and he starts to plan and strategize in his head.

He follows her through the doors to the building, and into the elevator. Inside the lift, he kisses her again, but not aggressively, not in a way that says that he already knows how this night is going to end. He isn't sure yet if he is in with a chance, and she isn't sure if tonight really is the night that she will let him in. The temptation though is really very strong, and it almost overwhelms her. There is something about a three-month rule that she remembers reading somewhere, but now that Trenton is walking into her apartment, she thinks that maybe it was just a load of nonsense anyway. What difference does it make whether you wait one month, or three months, as long as it is right?

And this really does feel right. Trenton hasn't put any pressure on her in any way, and she really starts to feel that there is something wrong with her. Maybe it is because she hasn't seen him with any black girls in the press, and maybe he just isn't attracted to her like that, but then again what would he be doing inside her apartment now. The questions and answers seem to overlap one another now, and she starts to think that this should happen before she loses her nerve.

But then again, what if she isn't ready for him to be with her like that? What if she just thinks she wants to, thinks she is ready? There is just one way to find out, but once they start down this road, there will be no turning back. There is no way to undo this once it is done, so she has to be very sure. She is, though, at least she thinks she is, and he is kissing her again on her lips, and on her neck, making her warm between her legs, so warm that her belly feels like it's on fire too.

She pulls away from him, offering him a drink. There must be a way to delay things just a little, just until she is sure. She pulls herself away from him completely and turns into the kitchen. He follows her and kisses the back of her head and neck while she pours them a glass of wine. There is nothing to hold him back, though, and as she sips her wine, he starts to undo her dress, needing to know if she is willing to let him into her world, completely.

As the dress drops to the floor, she steps out of it, still sipping on her wine. He hasn't touched his glass, working on her bra instead. He gets her completely naked while she continues to sip on her wine, finishing the contents of the glass and then considering her body too much, too late. She thinks of picking up his glass too but then thinks again, as his lips find her back, flooding her with kisses. He starts to kiss her back and then whispers in her ears for directions to the bedroom. She takes him by the hand and leads the way.

They arrive at the bedroom and Trenton has already released his cock from his jeans. He pushes her down on the bed, on her stomach, and leaves her lying there while he undresses himself completely. He doesn't want any help from her, and when he rolls a condom over his cock, the last one in his wallet, he starts to panic, sweating down his stomach. He goes over to the bed, and gets on it, dropping kisses up and down her back again, and then on her ass. Then he kisses the back of her thighs.

He positions himself on top of her, parting her legs with his waist. He really wants to be in her now, but he isn't sure if she is ready for him. He thinks of fingering her, but there is just something about her that makes him think that sticking his fingers inside her to check if she is wet might not be appropriate. He just has to trust his timing, trust that she will be ready when he finally goes into her. He teases the entrance to her pussy with his dick, and she tenses. Obviously, she is not yet ready for him.

Toni isn't ready at all, and she hates herself. She asks herself a million questions, the whys of it all a genuine concern for her, but she just needs to get over it. She really needs to be ready for him quickly, before she pisses him off and sends him packing. Somehow, though, she knows that he will not give up on her that easily. She will just need to be patient with herself, and allow for him to do what he must, what he wants to do, to get her ready.

He thrusts against the entry a little more, and then a little harder, and her pussy starts to give way. He doesn't say anything to her, not a whisper in her ear, nothing to distract her from what he is trying to achieve here. He senses that she is nervous, really nervous, and so he will not rush this at all. He will also not upset the apple cart by saying the wrong thing. He cannot lose the ground he is gaining, not now, not yet.

Trenton moves his cock up into her, finding her thankfully warm and wet. Her love pudding is delicious as it seems to wrap itself around his cock, inch by inch, making its way inside her. He really is in no hurry, but he wants to be inside her all the way, just to see how she can take him if she can take him completely. He knows that she has probably had bigger than him, but he needs to believe that she might not be able to handle him, just for his own ego.

As he thrusts his cock into her, it gets tighter and tighter. He knows that he is getting close to the back of her, to her depths, her limits, and so he pushes deeper, harder, just to make sure that he has filled every inch of her with himself. There is no way for him to see how much of his cock is still left on the outside of her cunt when he has reached the back of her pussy, but he convinces himself that it is a good couple of inches. Again this is just to feed his own ego.

Slowly he starts to thrust, moving his cock almost all the way out, and then all the way back inside her. Her pussy starts to sweat a little more and give a little more, and he is soon pumping into her steadily. He is careful to pull his cock almost all the way out, leaving just his head inside her, and then pushing all the way inside her. There is something about the completeness of this stroke that fills him with pleasure, her too. She starts to moan, softly at first, and then a little louder. She cannot help herself, moaning louder still, as he moves inside her all the way, almost extracting himself from her completely.

He kisses the back of her neck now, again, and then he starts to suck on the soft flesh behind her neck too. He thrusts faster into her, deeper, and then he eases up. Then again he is thrusting slowly into her, his lips and tongue finding the back of her neck over and over again. She wants to turn around, to look at him, but she can't. All she can do is put her head in her hands, and moan louder still into the sheets.

She lifts her ass, a little more, feeding him more of her pussy unintentionally, so that more of him disappears inside her. There seems to be enough of his cock left on the outside of her to make him comfortable, though, so he really is starting to feel more and more confident. Again he thrusts into her deeper, and harder, faster too, for the longest time, and then suddenly he stops, pulling his cock all the way out of her for the first time. He hangs there for a moment and then starts to ease his cock back into her, very slowly again.

There is a moment where he feels like he must be dreaming like he cannot possibly be inside Toni, but then he realizes that he is. He realizes that he has her exactly where he wants her and that she is very much enjoying him too, so he keeps at it. He keeps his cock inside her for a moment before he starts thrusting, really going for it this time, no intention to cum just yet, but every intention of bringing her to a beautiful orgasm. It works too, and soon enough she is blowing, beautifully, letting him know this by the soft pants escaping her mouth.

Trenton is pleased with himself, more than just a little. He keeps on thrusting into her slowly, wanting to cum now, but not sure if it is too soon yet. He knows that it isn't because she has had an orgasm, but he really feels the need to impress her. He really wants her to feel satisfied, more than just, and he really is able to control himself, knowing that his own climax can be postponed a little. He moves inside her slowly, so slowly, that he cunt starts to quiver.

He moves against this quivering, really measuring each stroke, each delicious stroke of his lengthy tool, so that she starts to give in to the possibility of a second orgasm. There is something about a second orgasm that she had no idea was on the cards, thinking that he was trying to bring himself to climax. But then she starts to feel the beginnings of a second orgasm, and she is really excited now. She tries to silence her groans now, but this is not possible. She stops trying, as he pumps steadily into her, bringing her closer still to an orgasm.

She starts to really feel him, in every part of her. The detachment that she felt earlier, pre the first orgasm, is now gone. There is something about being fucked by a guy from behind that can either make you feel like a whore if done badly or make you feel really loved if done properly. He is definitely on the way to doing it properly, making her feel more and more loved. There is nothing whorish about Trenton fucking her from behind. He is actually fucking her from above, and he is going so deep into her now that she is sure that she is going to blow at any moment.

But she doesn't, and this catches her completely off-guard. Trenton is not moving at all now, and she literally is grinding against his cock, willing herself over the edge. But he is removing his cock from inside her so that she has no choice but to watch as the orgasm that she was about to have slipped just out of her reach, just over the edge, without her. As he slips out of her completely, she is left longing, wanting him but knowing that she has lost him, at least for the moment.

Then he goes into her again, this time thrusting hard into her, making her feel like she is being pounded by a sledgehammer, deep inside herself. She likes it, really likes it, and so she lets herself be taken by him completely. Toni lifts her ass into him a little more, knowing that he is going to go for it now, that he has got to bring himself to a climax soon. But again he surprises her, and after pounding her close to orgasm, so close that she can taste it, and then nothing. Not from him, and certainly not for her.

He stops moving inside her now, but he keeps his cock inside her so that she feels like at least there is hope. She really had not anticipated a second orgasm or even expected one, but now that it is promised, now that it is clearly on the table, she really wants it. Trenton seems to have another idea, though, keeping it dangling in front of her like a carrot in front of a donkey. She almost cannot take it anymore.

Trenton kisses her again, on her upper back and neck, and in her hair. Then he kisses her on the sides of her face, and at last, finds her mouth. She had thought that because of their position, this would be impossible. She had not considered that Trenton is much taller than her and can, therefore, reach whatever part of her he wants to. Right now he wants her mouth, and finding it, he sends his tongue into it and enjoys it for the longest time. He doesn't move his cock at all, and she too doesn't grind against him anymore. She knows that she needs to let him do his thing, hoping that she will cum soon enough. He cannot go on forever too, she hopes.

But forever seems to be exactly what he is thinking of, as he is thrusting again into her, bringing her just close enough to an orgasm to get her to feel like she is going to cum but knowing somehow that she is not. She really doesn't, and she screams into the pillow, letting Trenton know that she is incredibly frustrated. He knows though that this must be in a very good way, so he just keeps on teasing her with the possibility of orgasm, just teasing him.

Then he is pounding her again. He is really giving it to her now, and he starts to feel like he is going to finally bring her over the edge. She lets herself believe it too, and as he moves in her in deep circles, he gets her on a collision course with an orgasm that even he knows would be cruel not to allow her to see through. He keeps at it and suddenly is on a collision course of his own. They are both on their way to climax now, and so there is no turning back for either of them today.

When they both cum together, it is beautiful. It is such a perfect conclusion to what has been a magnificent session. They really are both very satisfied, and so when they have started to come down from the orgasm, Trenton is still inside her, still hard. There is a moment where she thinks he is pulling his cock from her, but then he just sends it deeper into her, so that she almost forgets that he has already filled the condom with his semen and that he should really be over it by now.

When he moves out of her completely though she sighs a deep sigh of relief. She hadn't realized how completely stuffed she was, and now in the absence of this cock she is very aware of it. She breathes out through her mouth, and then she turns up to face him directly after he lifts himself off of her. Then they are facing each other, and he smiles at her. Then he kisses her, on her lips, and then on her forehead. Then he finds her lips again and draws her tongue into his mouth again.

They talk for hours, kissing and talking, and talking and kissing, and then they are quiet. The silence is comfortable, though so that there is nothing needed to fill the space left by this silence. Then she is on her back, and he is kissing her neck, before finding her mouth again, kissing her much longer this time, and then bringing her earlobes into his mouth, between his lips, and then his teeth. Then he finds her mouth for the umpteenth time and kisses her so long that her cunt is wet again. She really wants him inside her again, but he makes absolutely no move towards this.

Then she is suddenly shivering, his fingertips circling her belly button. He really is playing the piano on her belly, using his fingers, all the fingers on one hand, and then circling her belly button again. When he moves down onto her thighs, she feels that he might touch her cunt now, but again he doesn't. He just keeps on playing the piano on her thighs now, the same way that he was just playing on her belly, and this sends shards of pleasure into her again.

She curls up, trying to find a spot on his chest now, giving up the fight for a third orgasm. She knows that she should probably try and sleep soon, to avoid the pressure of conversation, but there is nothing uncomfortable when the conversation is absent. She cannot sleep, so she doesn't even try anymore. She tries not to sleep, but there are many times for her to think about sleeping now. Finding her spot on his chest, she settles into it and then just relaxes. The night moves from dreamlike state to wide awake, and Toni is very aware of his breathing. She knows that he is still awake, though, but still she has no need to speak to him.

When both of them are sleeping now, the night fills with the sounds of the city. The city really does sleep, because there are no people walking around in the streets below. But the city is vibrant, a series of hums and buzzes, and some horns, all coming together to sing them a beautiful lullaby, to make them feel like they are sleeping in a forest, a concrete forest of streetlights and sounds. This is really beautiful for the type of accommodation that this is.

Toni dreams of Trenton, and she really, really allows herself to believe that this is a real relationship. She has no doubt now, not when they have sealed the deal with the one thing that can make or break a relationship. They have made love, and Toni feels very vulnerable suddenly, she feels exposed, but not so much that she cannot sleep. She really sleeps deeply, so that Trenton is caught completely off-guard, but not so much that he also cannot sleep. They are wrapped in each other now so that they are very comfortable.

Trenton wakes up around 4 AM, needing the bathroom. She shifts her off his chest and goes to find it. As soon as he finds it, he closes the door and pees too loudly. He flushes the toilet and gets out of the space, moving to the kitchen, pouring himself a glass of wine, and taking it onto the terrace. He breathes in the night air and thinks about what has just gone down. He thinks about what they are really doing, satisfied by the sex, but really torn with the emotion of it all. There are really just a few things that are so different with Toni that he finds himself thinking more than just a little, about what this all means.

He goes back inside to the bedroom and gets back into bed. He moves closer to her, pulling Toni into him. She comes easily, and then he sends his arms around her. He runs his hands up and down her arms and then lingers on her hands. He takes the fingers on it between his and lets himself fall asleep again. He has not slept this easily in a very long time. It is beautiful. He just feels so comfortable in Toni's presence that there is nothing that keeps him back from sleeping.

Both of them are lost in their dreams now and in their thoughts. There are moments where they wake up but don't move, not wanting to wake the other. When they are awake together, the still don't say anything to each other, knowing that the sun will come up soon enough and pull them from their sleep. There are moments where they both want to speak to each other, but they still don't, just enjoying being in each other's presence. The moment is more than a little complete.

By 6 AM they are both so deep in sleep that there is nothing that can bring them out of their slumber. They just lie there, no longer holding, apart from each other in the bed but still close enough to each other to know that the other person is there. They really feel like they have slept forever, and Trenton really starts to feel his arousal growing with the rising sun. But then he is asleep again, remembering that he just had one condom in his jeans. Why the fuck did he bring just the one?

9

"Oh God, what have you done?' Toni asks herself, looking across her bed at the man still fast asleep in it. Trenton sleeps silently so that if his chest wasn't rising and falling, you would think he was dead. She pulls the sheets over her breasts, not really knowing why, but feeling that she has really done it now. Why didn't she say no, why not? Why did she not let him just drop her off and leave? There is no going back now, and Trenton is waking up. Oh shit!!!

He opens his eyes and looks at me. Toni cannot hide herself from him either now, looking at him at the exact moment that his eyes open. "Good morning beautiful..." he says, rather predictably. Toni isn't sure if it is his intention to sound so contrived. She responds although she cannot even hear the sound of her response coming out of her mouth. There just seems to be a very loud buzz between her ears. In fact, if she wasn't looking at Trenton directly now, she would shake her head to free herself from this buzzing.

He comes up to her, meeting her face midair, kissing her before she can protest. She wishes suddenly that she had showered and brushed her teeth, flossed and used mouthwash before Trenton woke up. But it is too late now, and their lips meet. She hopes for a second that he won't put his tongue in her mouth, what with the morning breath situation, but before she can pull away, his tongue is inside her mouth, moving around in there, literally brushing her teeth. She cringes, but kisses him back, albeit rather tentatively.

Then he moves himself from her, his eyes on hers still, looking through her discomfort, and finding it very cute. He holds her face, tenderly, between his fingers, and then in his hands, still looking at her. The sun catches her eyes just right at that moment, and he notices that they are a translucent hazel. They are very beautiful indeed, and suddenly seem to take on another life. There seems to be much more hiding behind them than you would see if you just looked at her, without attempting to see through her.

Toni suddenly feels very vulnerable, more so than she did last night. She really didn't feel any vulnerabilities last night, though, mostly because she noticed that Trenton too felt awkward. But one thing is clear now, though, they have actually slept together. There is no turning back now, and nothing that can undo what has now been done. Toni thinks about what happened last night again, Trenton too, although for different reasons. Toni is wondering what this means for them, while Trenton is still consumed with thoughts of whether or not he was actually good enough. His inadequacies suddenly come to the surface and flush his face red.

There is something about the aftermath of the night before that leaves them both feeling more than a little strange. Strange in a good way, but also not. There is a conflict of emotions in them that dance like night and day inside both of them, and this dance really turns into a tango. There are things that stir inside them and then go to sleep, moving up and down in them like emotional yo-yos. The words cannot come to any of them now, as they look through each other again, unable to speak to one another.

Trenton kisses her again, to break the tension, to eliminate the awkwardness. She really kisses him back now, really going for it. Toni is the one letting her tongue into Trenton's mouth now, also realizing that the silence was starting to feel very awkward, needing to break this unspoken tension. They lose themselves in one another now, both of them feeling like they did last night, just before they finally surrendered to the passions. Before long it is obvious that they are about to make love again, and so Toni closes her eyes, knowing that she almost needs the confirmation of this second escapade.

Toni thinks of last night, going

through it in stages, like flash images through her head. She does this without skipping a beat, though, kissing Trenton with as much attention to detail as though he were the only thing on her mind. She isn't here, though, not completely, working through last night's events in her head, thinking about everything that she did, and didn't do. She really needs to know what she can do differently now, what she can do better. She really needs to make this morning session better.

Frame by frame, she realizes that last night she wasn't very active. She let Trenton take full control of the situation, and let him make love to her. She did nothing of her own accord, probably because she was surprised by the event, and also probably because she wasn't very sure of herself, not lacking in confidence, though, but certainly not sure of Trenton. Sure they had gone on a few dates, and yes he made her laugh. But he did not do or say anything that could have prepared her for last night. And now it was happening again, and again she is at a loss as to what to do.

Toni goes onto her back again,

Trenton kissing her breasts now, and then sucking her nipples. She arches her back so that her nipples are inside his mouth more, enjoying the feeling of his lips on her breasts, his teeth on her nipples. All of his mouth seems to be taking full advantage of every part of her tits now, something she doesn't remember him doing last night. She doesn't even remember him sucking her tits at all last night, and so she really gives herself to this beautiful moment, knowing somehow that it is the very first time.

She really enjoys the way he seems to taste every part of her breasts too, taking his time on what were previously just mounds on her chest. Toni really has a new appreciation for her tits. She almost forgets the rest of her body for a moment, for as long as Trenton is working on her breasts. But Trenton has not forgotten about his body, and while his mouth is busy on her chest, he takes a hand to his erection, stroking it lightly. He really wants to be inside her again, but she is enjoying the breast action, so he will not deny her this pleasure.

After the longest time, Trenton works

down her belly, to her belly button, where again he lingers. He sends his tongue into her deep belly button, and moves it around in circles, slowly, going deeper into her belly button so that she again loses herself in the moment. He really knows how to work the ridges of her body, getting into her grooves with just his tongue, but sending the feeling through her that he is touching her with every part of himself.

Suddenly she panics, as his lips move off her naval, into the space between her belly button and her clit, thinking a million thoughts. She hasn't showered yet, so the remnants of last night's tryst are still on her, in her. Her pussy is aching with the anticipation that his mouth will at any second now settle on it, but he mustn't, he can't, she thinks to herself. Oh lord, what will it taste like, what will it feel like in his mouth? She is having an anxiety attack now, seriously, and she tries to cross her legs over each other.

But there is no way for her to bring her legs closed, it is too late now, Trenton's face already between her legs. His tongue licks her clit hard, and this sends shards of pleasure all the way through her, into her legs, up her belly, into her breasts, and into her head. He licks it again and then sucks on it hard. He is kissing it now, really kissing it, licking, and sucking, and then nibbling on it. Just as she gets used to one sensation he is hitting her with another, then another. She wraps her legs around his back, then on his neck and head, and pulls him deeper into her.

There is nothing that she can do about how she tastes or even how she smell now. He is already there, in it to win it, and he is really going for it. He must enjoy the taste of her because even when she has a mild unexpected orgasm, he is still sucking on her. He really is eating her out now, but not all of her, not yet. Trenton is just focusing on her clit, and he is turning it into a small ball of electricity with his mouth.

When he finally goes for her cunt, he still doesn't just stick his tongue in there. He licks her lips gently, and then sends the tip of his tongue in-between these two flaps, tickling the hole, just tickling it. Then he pushes his tongue into the hole, just a little, before he takes it out, licking her lips again. Again he inserts just the tip of his tongue into her and moves it around the entrance to her just for a moment, before, yet again, he is just licking her lips. The anticipation of full entry starts to build inside her.

He gets half his tongue into her now, and fucks her with this half, gently. He goes so gently that she thinks that he is almost scared of going all the way. But the deliberateness of it is beautiful, and she really just enjoys it. As soon as he goes all the way inside her, she again feels like she is having an orgasm, but she doesn't. She just feels like she is caught between orgasms now, and eventually, she has no choice but to surrender to this limbo. It is deliciously frustrating.

Trento really goes for her depths now, sucking the shit out of her pussy, pulling her closer and closer to a real orgasm. But just as she feels she might blow, he licks the outside of her cunt as if to say to her 'not yet.' She goes absolutely insane now, and she wraps her legs tighter around his head. He lets her, sending his tongue deep into her again, licking the walls of her pussy dry and wet all at once. She again feels close, but she knows that he will not let her cum just yet. She is okay with this.

After pulling on his own cock a little harder, he lets it go, bringing himself too close. He puts his hands on her knees and pushes down, parting her legs. He now has full, uncompromising access to her pussy, and he really starts to devour it. There is no need for him to hold her back now, no need for him to keep her from having an orgasm, no need. She starts to have an orgasm, so intense, that she literally sprays the inside of his mouth with the contents of her pussy. Still, he doesn't skip a beat, sucking harder on her pussy, drinking every drop of this spray.

When he finally removes his mouth from her, he licks his lips. Then he drops kisses on her cunt, all over it, especially on her clit. She shudders, really shakes now, and Trenton holds her legs down. He runs his fingers up from her knees, onto her thighs, and then he is parting her cunt lips with his fingers, sending his tongue into the space again, just for effect. And this is really effective because she is having another orgasm quickly, something that she doesn't expect, but loves.

Trenton works up her belly again, with his mouth, and again he finds her breasts. He kisses them lightly before sucking them, bringing his cock against her still-recovering pussy. He rubs himself against her, and his dick starts to ache and pulse, really wanting in her now. There are few things that would stop him from just going into her right now, and one of them is the fact that he doesn't have a condom on. Where the fuck are the condoms? He remembers the one that he took out of his jeans last night, but he only remembers this one. What if he has no protection? Will she risk fucking him bareback? He doesn't need to ask.

Toni knows that he wants to get inside her, and she knows that she will not risk pregnancy. She leans over to the side table and opens the drawer, Trenton stopping for a moment to see what she is doing before returning to her breasts. She searches the draw and then pulls out a strip of three condoms. She hands them to him, searching for his hand under the cover, her eyes closed now, as she really enjoys the feeling of him on her tits again. She knows that it won't be long now before he is inside her.

Trenton gets out a condom when he eventually moves his mouth off her, and he rolls it on his cock without even looking. He is obviously skilled at this, doing it on the regular. He also seems to do it with one hand, which Toni cannot help but find impressive. She wonders why he doesn't seem interested in having her mouth on him. Perhaps he doesn't think that she can suck cock. Perhaps there is something about her that says that she is too much of a prude to have a dick in her mouth.

This is of course not the case. She doesn't mind dick in mouth. In fact, she really enjoys it. There are things about lovemaking that she really didn't know until now, and she is glad that Trenton introduced her to these things. Now she has a reference for all her future lovemaking, something to draw from in order to make sure that the experience is great for her too. But cock-sucking is something that she is really good at, she thinks. And she would like the opportunity to show Trenton just how good she is.

But this will have to wait, though, because Trenton is again rubbing his now-wrapped cock against her pussy, nudging against her clit, and against the entrance. Then he starts to ease himself into her, slowly, deliciously. She doesn't move, not wanting to upset his rhythm as he enters her. He seems to be enjoying the entry too much. So she just lies there until he is snuggly all the way inside her. Trenton exhales hard now, as he settles into her, really very pleased that he has had the patience to wait for this exact moment. There is something about making love to Toni that makes him want to make it all about her.

He breathes in now, pulling his cock almost all the way out of her. Then he starts to thrust slowly, in no rush, no hurry to get anywhere, just happy to be inside her again. She feels almost better than she did last night, and he is in heaven. Slowly he fucks her, watching her face closely as she adjusts to his cock. He knows now, now that he can see her face, that his cock is a perfectly acceptable size. His inadequacies fade fast now, and he knows that he has her where he wants her.

Trenton really focuses now, knowing that he needs to make this good. He remembers everything about last night, everything, but not in as much detail as he would like to. He feels like this is the first time that he is really making love to Toni, with his full senses. He isn't wired. He hasn't been for a while now. Actually, he hasn't even thought of cocaine, which is strange for him. And he is also sober, not even the slightest hint of a hangover. All his energy is with him now, and he has the focus and precision of a heart surgeon.

There is nothing clinical about their lovemaking, though. He just pays attention to detail, to every detail, knowing that the most important thing for him is that she feels good. Needless to say, he is also feeling very good. Very, very good. But he tries very hard not to lose himself, wanting to bring her to a beautiful finish. He thrusts into her deeper now and then pauses. Then he slowly pulls half of himself out of her before plunging himself into her all the way again.

Over and over again he gives her the full measure of his power, and over and over again he draws beautiful, soulful moans from her. He too is moaning, as much in response to the sounds that she is making, as to the pleasure that he is deriving from digging into her depths. The sun is beautiful on his back too, the covers off him now, so far down his ass that he feels the kisses of the sun on his butt cheeks. He transfers this heat into her with his cock.

He starts to move into her in small circles now, sensual deep circles that make her groan now. Trenton starts to think of new ways to make love to her, but these deep circles bring her close to orgasm, so close that he wouldn't dream of stopping now. He keeps at it, for about ten minutes, and then when she starts to cum, he smiles at her, her eyes closed, and he kisses her eyelids. Then he brings himself to a beautiful orgasm, and leaves his cock inside her, falling on her with his full weight, closing his eyes too now as he kisses her on her lips.

He doesn't lose his erection for a minute, and even when he pulls his cock from her, it is still rock hard. He uses both hands to remove the condom, and sort it out. He pulls some tissue from her side table and wraps the condom in it. Then he replaces the condom with a new one and goes into her again. He cannot resist this. Starting to fuck her harder, he cannot hold himself back any longer, suddenly everything about him. There is just no way for him to control himself anymore.

Harder and harder he goes into her, and she seems to enjoy it even more. Trenton knows that they are really starting to gel now, really gelling, and so he can keep on fucking her harder, and so he does. Deeper and deeper he goes inside her, and she is suddenly on her way to another orgasm. He beats her to it, though, much against his better judgment, against his own will. But still he is hard, and still, he goes into her over and over again, bringing her closer still. She parts her legs a little more, letting him in a little deeper.

She blows at last, just in time too, because Trenton is more than a little worn out now. Never before has he paid so much attention to the woman underneath him. He watches her eyes, her face, making sure that he has satisfied her completely before he stops moving, keeping himself inside her, though. He moves slowly from side to side as he loses his erection. Limp now, he keeps himself inside her for a moment longer before he slips his cock out of her. He has to sort out the condom before it slips off his limp cock and he messes her bed.

He rolls off the bed and pulls the condom off. He takes the other condom from her bedside table and then goes to the bathroom. She gathers herself sufficiently and then she too slips from the bed, following him to the bathroom. When she gets there, he has thrown the condoms in the toilet, and he is pissing over the floating mess. Then he flushes the lot down the toilet, and moves away, giving Toni the space she needs to pee as well. He looks at her sitting on the toilet, and then he comes closer to her, kissing her on the mouth again. Then he turns to the bath and opens the taps.

Toni watches him as he pours some bubble bath into the water, shaking it around to make sure that the bubbles form quickly. Toni cannot help but brush her teeth now, although they seem to be so far beyond that it feels like they have been in a relationship forever. Trenton closes the taps and then comes over to where Toni is rinsing her mouth now. He takes her toothbrush, using it to brush his own teeth too. This is really feeling like forever kind of love.

They sit in the bath for the longest time, talking about everything under the sun, then talking about nothing, just kissing. After their long, languid bath, they order breakfast in, and enjoy it, along with each other's company. They talk until way afternoon, kissing some more, no need to make love anymore. Not that they don't want to, but they don't want to jinx it, not wanting to become the victims of overkill. When Trenton finally leaves Toni's apartment, she isn't sure what to make of what just happened. One thing is clear, though, clearer than it was at the beginning of this morning's activities, and that is that there really is now no going back from here.

Trenton arrives home, and his head is flooded with thoughts of Toni. He really likes her, and he has had her now, really had her. He knows that the sex can only get better, more adventurous, more intriguing. But what is uppermost on his mind is what this means for their relationship. He has never been able to commit to anything, not able to really commit. But now he starts to think that he might just have met his match. He isn't sure, though, and this uncertainty is what has him in a tailspin.

Toni too is consumed with thoughts of Trenton. They have started dating, much against her better judgment. And now they have slept together, more than once, and she isn't sure how she feels about this. She isn't sure about anything. Maybe it was all just an elaborate plan to get her into bed. If so, then it has worked. What does this mean for her now, though, she wonders? She wonders how this new turn of events will affect her work with Live Records.

Maybe she should have slept with CJ, or Cole even, anybody but the boss. She knows that these things never end well, for anybody. She picks up her guitar, and she strums out a few chords. She sings to herself, loudly on the balcony, the sun making its moves in the sky from one side of it to another. Thoughts raced like wildfire through her head, and she wonders again what this will mean tomorrow at the office. She wonders how much of what happened here will make it into the boys-night conversation, or who Trenton will discuss her with tonight even.

Well, there is nothing that she can do to take back what has happened, not now. She goes out for a drink, just to clear her head, and to get herself in the frame of mind that she thinks will be required of her tomorrow if it goes south. How can it, though, how? Trenton seemed sincere when they went on the few dates that they did, and he seemed to really pay attention to her when they made love. But now that they have made love, the ball really is in his court. She wonders how it will play out as she walks into a pub near her home and makes her way onto the terrace, isolating herself from the world, left alone with her thoughts.

10

Trenton doesn't come into the studio for four days after they make love, and this drives Toni a little bit crazy. He doesn't call her and makes no attempt to see her at all. This really bothers her, really it does. She cannot even concentrate on anything the CJ says, her guitar straining more than strumming too. There is no pressure for her to deliver anything musically, not yet, but even though, there is really nothing forthcoming. There is nothing musical that escapes her, and this bothers her even more so than Trenton's apparent disappearing act.

Come Friday, Toni really is concerned. She thinks that it was probably her fault for being so naïve, but now that it has affected her ability to work, this is really a problem. She could have handled being snubbed by anybody else, anybody. Trenton is a whole other story, though, and she finds that she really wants his approval. He seems to have moved on from her, though, and this is something that really doesn't go down well with her.

Why did she sleep with him? Why did she fall for his charm, and for his advances? Surely she isn't so blind so as not to have really seen what she thought she saw in him? Toni really considers herself to be a good judge of character, or at least she thought she was before now. She has always been a good reader of people, always, but now everything that she thinks she knew about herself is remarkably challenged. She cannot shake it too, feeling more and more useless, Friday not coming quickly enough for her really. At least there are two days that she doesn't have to be in the Studio, waiting for

Trenton to not appear.

This is another thing that gets to her too. She knows from what she has heard around the studio that Trenton has never shown any sort of interest in any other artist, not the way he has with her. And now that they have slept together, all interest seems to be lost. There is only one thing to make of this change, and that is that he has got what he wants from her, and has moved on, scratching her off like an item on his to-do list.

This isn't too far from what is happening too, not too far from the truth. Trenton is conflicted. He has always been a playboy, and he doesn't understand why he has let Toni get under his skin the way she has. Surely he isn't ready to settle down, and certainly not with the much younger girl, who is nothing like him. He comes from good stock, as he has always been told. And she, certainly, does not. There can be no future here, he thinks.

The fact that he is even thinking about this is a problem for him. Why is he even considering the future with her, he wonders? Yes, he enjoyed fucking her, he really did. And when he left her house that day he thought that he would see her again that evening, or the next day the latest. But now he is thinking about things, really thinking about things, and the general vibe of how things are between them suddenly doesn't sit well with him. This should really be, as it has always been, a one-fuck-wonder situation. But he finds himself thinking of Toni more than he should, and so he decides to get himself out of the headspace that he is in.

It is Friday night, and two very different things are happening on two very opposite ends of LA. In Malibu, Trenton is busy entertaining some of his friends, again doing more lines of cocaine than is practical. He is also drinking too much champagne, and way too many vodka shots. He is starting to feel like his old self again, and he is more than a little comfortable with himself again. There is something about the familiarity of it all that really makes him very happy.

Toni is alone in her downtown apartment. She is also drinking champagne, but alone in the dark. This has really been a strange week, and she is wondering if she shouldn't perhaps go over to Trenton's house and ask him what the hell is going on. She really struggles with this too, and the more she drinks, the more like an actual idea it is starting to sound like. But she cannot bring herself to rock up at his house drunk. She isn't really, though, but not her usual self, not her usual controlled self.

She walks out onto her rooftop garden and looks over her view of the city's night skyline. She sips more of the champagne from the flute in her glass and then breathes in the night air. There is just one thing for her to do, although it is very early, and that is to get to bed. Sleep will come easy because of the bubbles, but not before she has soaked in the bath with a glass of red wine. She takes another glass with her to bed, and fiddles on her Blackberry for a moment, just until she has finished the wine. Then she snuggles into bed and goes to sleep.

Trenton is having a great time on the Malibu end of town, though. He is really wired now, and the alcohol is lubricating him enough to make him feel a little amorous. He also feels nothing about the fact that he has another women's mouth on his cock now, a paler mouth, and she is really very pretty. Trenton doesn't know her name, though, but there is the whole night for him to figure out how to ask her for this little detail. He has really forgotten about the conflicting feelings that he had about Toni, and he focuses all his energies on the women at the party, particularly the enthusiastic filly sucking his cock.

He is in his bedroom, his friends still out by the pool enjoying themselves. He too is also enjoying himself, very much. Trenton really has all but forgotten about the way he was feeling earlier this week, the confusion associated with Toni, and this is an incredible relief for him. He was really starting to feel a little out of his depth, but now he is back. He thrusts his cock a little deeper into the woman's mouth, and he is glad that it is hard. At least he will fuck her mouth until he sprays the inside of her mouth with his semen.

He watches as she moves eagerly on his meat, listening to the sounds of his friends by the pool. There really was no need for him to rush this, but he really felt that if he didn't do it now, his resolve might fail him. Why the hell was he still struggling with this? Why did thoughts of Toni creep up on him still, unexpectedly? So here he was, with his dick moving in and out of the mouth in the pretty face on her knees, with his tool in her hands too, just so that she can get a grip on it.

Trenton really pushes passed the thoughts of Toni now, still hanging menacingly in the back of his mind. He manages too and keeps fucking into the mouth, deeper, harder, closing his eyes. Thoughts of Toni again come up into his head, he imagines that it was her who was actually sucking his cock. He realizes that she hasn't even had her mouth on him, but that seems moot right now. He has tasted her where it matters, and he can get his cock sucked by anyone on any night.

Hell, he can get any pussy he wants, any time he wants. He knows this. This has been his life for the last few years, and even before, even when his family was still alive. There is absolutely no need for him to change now, not now, not yet. There is no reason for him to give up what has worked for him for the longest time. Why would he even think of giving it up for Toni too? Shit, he is thinking of Toni again. He has to shake her from his head, from his cock.

He lifts the woman off his cock now and takes her panties down. He lifts her skirt and throws her on the bed. By the time he gets to her, he has rolled a condom down his shaft, ready to mount her. He does and starts pounding hard. He really goes for it, really, really does, and he has absolutely no concern for the woman underneath him. He fucks her so hard that she starts to scream, placing a hand on either of his hipbones, just to slow him down a little bit. Trenton does slow down, but he moves her hands off his hips and holds them against the bed.

She isn't screaming because she is in pain either. She is screaming because she is already cumming, and she tried, in vain to slow him down. Now that she has cum, though, she has no choice but to wait for Trenton to cum. And the wait is long. The wait is very long indeed. He fucks her steadily for a good forty-five minutes before he eventually fills the condom with his seed. He pulls out of her immediately and goes to the bathroom to sort out the condom. When he comes out, she has gone downstairs already, obviously not feeling the need to do any cleaning of herself, or maybe she just used one of the other bathrooms. He really doesn't care.

When he gets down to the other guests again, she is already on another man, kissing him, running her fingers up and down his cock over his shorts. Not to worry, though, this is that sort of party. Everybody is free to do what they want, and certainly who they want. They will swap partners two or three times before the sun comes up, and by noon tomorrow, all will have been forgotten. Again, when Trenton wakes up in the morning, not that he has really slept, he doesn't know the name of the girl who finds herself in his bed.

A woman he does know is Toni though, and she is standing in his doorway. He thinks he must be imagining things, and he closes his eyes and shakes his head vigorously from side to side. When he opens them again, she is still standing in his doorway, two coffees and a box of croissants in her hands. Who the fuck let her in, he wonders, at a loss as to what to say, looking from her to the woman still asleep next to him, her ass in the air, outside the covers. She is perfect in every way, and she is also white, so Toni knows that this is probably what made all the difference.

She really doesn't know what to say, everything clearly spread out in front of her. She doesn't need an explanation, and she suddenly doesn't know what she was thinking coming here. The resolve that she had the night before not to come was a good idea, she should have just gone with that. What is it about this morning that made her feel the need to get a cab all the way out her, unannounced, and not even allow him the opportunity to at least meet her downstairs and hide this woman from view? But then again, why would he have to hide her, she asks herself? Trenton owes her absolutely no explanation, and as she makes her way down the drive, calling a cab, she wills herself not to cry. She cannot help it, though.

All the way along the beach she cries, hating herself for it but not able to hold herself back. She looks at the houses peeping just over the cliff faces, some of them clear in their outline, and she suddenly sees her life as it could be, flash before her. There are dreams that can only come to you in your moments of deepest despair, and right now she feels nothing but despair. She also feels hopeful, and suddenly very ambitious. She takes out her phone, and starts Googling estate agents in the Malibu area, knowing that she cannot yet afford a place in this prime real estate, but needing suddenly to see what is out there.

She makes appointments with several of them, for the next afternoon, Sunday, perfectly acceptable in the world of estate agents, and she goes straight home. Toni makes herself a beautifully consolatory lunch, that becomes dinner, and she opens a bottle of wine. She loses herself in her drink and tries not to think about what happened that morning. She tries in vain to free her mind of the image of the sexy white woman sleeping on

Trenton's bed and the look on his face.

Toni takes her phone now and turns it off. She doesn't want to drunk text Trenton or call him. She wants nothing to do with him anymore. She can work with him, she has to. Toni also knows that there is no way for them to break her contract, so as long as she delivers, then there really is no way for them to break the agreement that is already signed. She just has to deliver on her end of the bargain, and she will get paid. Toni makes up her mind to do just that.

She does hate the fact that this sudden epiphany came at the expense of her virtue. No, she was certainly no virgin, but the feeling of being used settles over her in waves, and she feels sick to her stomach. She really hates it. But they do say that success is the best form of revenge, so she just has to be successful, and she has to be exceptionally civil towards Trenton, going forward, and that's that. She finishes making her lunch and settles into her third glass of wine, looking over the view of the city that she has, enjoying how day becomes night, but still hating the feeling of exposure to

Trenton. She really let her guard down.

After two bottles of wine solo and a rather technical pasta dish, she is ready for bed. She has even forgotten her phone now, and she just showers and jumps into bed. Tomorrow will be a good day for her, she tells herself. Tomorrow she will go and look at houses, firmly establishing her dream in her head. She remembers what they said in The Secret, many years ago when she watched it, that you need to get yourself to walk through the house of your dreams, test drive the car of your dreams, just to get a sense of what it will feel like to own these things. This is what she intends to do.

Sunday comes rather quickly but finds her well rested. She gets up and goes for a brisk walk around the block, several times, just to get into the day. She has a smile on her face, knowing that at least now she has a plan. There is something about knowing, knowing what the game is, what people are playing at, what their agendas have been, that is strangely liberating. After she gets back and has a quick shower, she takes a cab to the restaurant that she had arranged to meet the first estate agent at. She orders an omelet and juice, knowing that she has arrived early enough to finish eating by the time the agent arrives.

When the agent walks into the restaurant, she is all glam. Toni too is rather glamorous, looking every bit like young Hollywood, even though she doesn't necessarily feel like it. After a quick chat and coffee, they head out and start the viewings. The houses are every bit as luxurious on the inside as they appear on the outside. She loves them, all of them, and soaks in the feeling of ownership that comes from fooling yourself into believing that you are just one check-signing away from owning this place. It is the same with all the houses, even with the other estate agents. By the time she is done viewing the last house she gets the estate agent to drop her at the Jalapeño again, even though she is tired. She just needs to be out.

Walking into the space around 6 PM, she feels very confident. She is greeted with a recognition that comes with being there before with Trenton and CJ, and she milks it. She decides to milk this for everything that it is worth, starting today. She also decides that she doesn't need the complications of sleeping with the boss anyway, and she can and will get over the fact that Trenton won. This must have been a very elaborate game for him, though, she thinks to herself. He actually pretended to date her. He really went all out just to get her.

This sort of makes her feel better, and she orders a drink. She looks around the restaurant too, not sitting on the terrace, but sitting in the main hall of the space, so that she can see all the patrons as they come in and go out of the space. She isn't looking for anything in particular, but if someone notices her, and if someone comes over and starts talking to her, then she will not be against this at all. In fact, it might be just what she needs to get over what has recently happened with Trenton.

After a few drinks, and a few eyes thrown her way, she starts to feel uncomfortable, though. It is almost as though she would be cheating on Trenton, a feeling that she cannot shake. She holds her ground, though, staying seated, not wanting any of these men to come up to her now, but not wanting to leave, feeling like she cannot give Trenton so much power over her. But he has, and he doesn't even know it. He has no idea the sheer trauma that he is causing Toni still, even after what she saw in his bedroom the morning before.

Trenton too has been thinking of the morning that Toni walked into his bedroom. What the hell was she doing there? What made her feel like she could just show up at his house like that? He tries to think about everything that was said the night the made love, and the morning they made more love. Shit, he was a real jerk. He spoke to her, spoke with her as if they were building something, or at least starting something. He knows he did, and he also knows that there was no need for him to be such an asshole. There were cleaner ways of getting into Toni's pants.

He really lost himself for a moment. Or is it that he is lost now, and that she found him, that she really saw him for who he really is. Maybe, just maybe, Toni saw what everybody else wouldn't, what they couldn't. He feels even more like a douchebag now, and he goes to get into his car. He needs to speak to her, needs to say something to her, but even as he drives towards her apartment, he doesn't know exactly what this is. How the hell does he explain his behavior to her?

And what if she doesn't want to hear his explanation? What if she has written him off already? This is LA after all, and he knows, as he is sure she knows, the nature of the game that they are in. The music industry is wrought with such trysts, and so it is almost expected, almost acceptable. He knows somehow though that Toni will not accept the status quo, and that she wouldn't have slept with him if she hadn't believed that they were building something solid. She just wasn't that kind of girl.

When he gets to her apartment, she isn't there. He cannot bring himself to leave, though, cannot bring himself to move away from the building, pressing and repressing the buzzer. Maybe she is there, and maybe she just doesn't want to speak to him. He doesn't blame her, but also his resolve to speak to her grows with every minute that passes.

He keeps his finger on the buzzer for the longest time, looking up at the windows he thinks are hers. He walks away from the building now, and looks up, counting the floors, guessing at which windows belong to her. He thinks of shouting for her but returns instead to the buzzer.

Toni really isn't there, though, although she really wishes she was. Not that she knows that Trenton is acting a fool in front of her building, but he really is the only man on her mind. She hates that he has really crept into that place in her that she was saving for the man that she really loves. But she has, and she doesn't know what to do about it. She orders another drink, and although she is not getting drunk, she really wishes that she was.

When she leaves the restaurant, she takes a cab just outside and gives him her address. She rests her head on the side paneling of the door and watches the lights go by. Too soon she is home, and just before she gets out of the cab, she sees Trenton, and she freezes. What the hell is he doing her, what has he come to say? She really doesn't have the energy for what he has to say, doesn't want to hear it. Whatever he has to say to her she can hear it in the studio tomorrow, in front of witnesses. It will be easier to ignore him in the presence of other people.

Toni watches him, pressing the buzzer, watches him screaming up to her imagined window. Everything in her wants to get out of the cab, to hear what he has to say. She holds on to the door handle, though, locking herself in the cab. The driver looks from her to Trenton, and he seems to know what is going on. She really looks conflicted, but the driver knows better than to ask her what is going on. He doesn't turn off the car, though, just look at her through the rearview mirror.

Trenton sits down on the sidewalk and holds his head in his hands. She isn't sure if he is drunk, suddenly wishing that she was more inebriated. Fuck, she really doesn't need this complication in her life, not now. She isn't sure if he is coming to tell her off for just showing up at his house, or if he is here to say what she actually wishes that he is. She really doesn't know how she will handle it, either way. Shit, she shouldn't have slept with him. She shouldn't have dated him if that is even what they were doing.

She rehearses a conversation in her head, knowing that she needs to stand her ground, and let him know how she feels, and what this has done to her. She plans on the best way to tell him that she doesn't need the complications of sleeping with the boss, and also that she doesn't have the strength to try and fix him, to try and get him to love her right. After taking a deep breath, and paying the taxi driver, she gets out of the cab, knowing that her resolve will fail her as soon as she is standing in front of him. As soon as he just says the right thing, she will forget everything that she has already practiced saying to him in the car.

Here goes nothing, she thinks, walking across the road to where he is looking with intention at the nothing that is lying on the ground...

11

"What was that?" Trenton asks her, as soon as he sees her walking across the road.

"What?" Toni asks in return, surprised by his tone. She thought that he would have come to explain himself, or to apologize, but clearly not.

"Just showing up at my house like that..." he continues, not sure himself of where this sudden anger comes from.

"Oh, that... I'm sorry... It won't happen again..." Toni responds, leaving him still sitting on the sidewalk, needing to create distance between herself and him before she says something that she will not be able to take back.

She walks into her building and straight towards the elevator. She doesn't see that Trenton has slipped through the door, which takes just a second too long to close. He follows her down the hallway, without saying anything. As soon as she steps into the elevator, though, he follows her in it and presses for the penthouse. Toni really doesn't know what to make of this situation. She feels trapped, almost as though she were suddenly forced to have something to say.

Nothing comes to her mind, though, and she looks at Trenton, square in the eyes. She searches for something, anything that will give her an indication of what to say, what to think, what to feel. The confusion of all these things comes up in the pit of her stomach and starts to curdle. She thinks she might throw up. Toni swallows hard. The elevator seems to take forever to get to the top floor, and the silence is so thick and loud inside the lift that she can hear her thoughts as if they were whispers. Loud whispers. When the doors finally slide open she feels like the relief of it might knock her out completely. She needs to get away from Trenton.

He follows her to her front door, though, still silent, still saying nothing. He looks her, the malice from moments earlier seeming to dissipate with the sun, now setting fully. It actually almost looks like rain, but this is LA and it hardly ever rains. When it does, though, it is dramatic and beautiful. It almost looks like it might happen now, even through the night sky. But it doesn't. She walks through to the doors leading onto the terrace, and the walks out on it. Trenton follows her.

Now he looks confused. A hint of the menace returning to his eyes briefly, and then disappearing. He is sending so many mixed signals that she starts to feel like she is on a rollercoaster. "What do you want from me?" she asks, eventually. "I said I was sorry, and I know that I shouldn't have come to your house. There really is nothing more that I can say…" She looks at how he will catch this ball that she has thrown back into his court with both hands.

"I know you're sorry...And you should be..." Trenton replies, leaving her alone on the rooftop terrace for the time it takes him to get to her fridge, help himself to a beer, and walk back out, looking past her at the city lights. Toni knows that she needs to get him out of here, but how? What can she say to him that will let him know that she really doesn't want him here when this is in fact exactly what she wants? Again her stomach is curdling with confusion.

Trenton runs his fingers along the length of his cock, a look on his face that says 'I'm a bad boy bitch and you know you want me.' Toni shudders, not believing that she actually fell for all of his crap during their 'dating' phase. She really thought that she was a better judge of character than that, but there really is no use crying over spilled milk, or wine. She remembers the open bottle of red in her living room, and now she is the one escaping for a drink. She joins Trenton on the terrace again, and notices, not that she is trying to hard not to, that he now has a massive erection.

She waits for him to finish his beer, sipping her wine slowly, so that she can watch Trenton with the distraction of her glass. She lets her eyes linger on the rod formation in his pants again, and he catches her stare. Unfortunately for Trenton, Toni isn't drunk enough to explain fucking him again, not after the way he treated her, and certainly not after what happened at his house, with that girl. When he drops his bottle on the table, she finally sees her gap and asks him to leave. To her surprise, he does, without putting up any sort of resistance. He just bites his bottom lip and looks over her breasts as she holds her front door open for him.

Toni works hard at the studio the next day, really hard. But it is forced, and CJ notices this. He knows too why, knowing what must have happened between her and Trenton, and hating the fact that his boss, and hers, was such an asshole. Could he not have waited until after she was album ready to bed her? Now he has to deal with an artist who has lost some of her spark before her career has even managed to catch a flame. Yes, he also had designs on her, but he was more patient than Trenton. He doesn't even know how to ask her about it, not sure if talking about it will help.

CJ is a little disappointed though that he didn't get the first chance with Toni, almost hating the fact that she decided to go with the white man first. Surely there is an unspoken rule about brothers getting first dibs on blackberries? Surely! But obviously not, Trenton having the fact that he is the boss going for him. CJ isn't sure what Toni thought would happen, though, because Trenton's reputation was no secret, from anyone. Everybody had something to say about him, and they were not the most flattering statements.

After this session, he lets Toni go home, not knowing what else to say to her. She committed to an album too soon, and now there were schedules in place, and plans made. The pressure to deliver was brought into the situation by nobody else but Toni herself, and now there was no turning back. She needs to get over Trenton and his penis quickly so that she can return to her old self. There was something incredibly soulful about Toni pre-Trenton. Now she just seems to be a real basket case. CJ will have to find a way to bring her back, though and fast.

Toni knows too that she is not herself, and she hates it. She should never have let Trenton into her life like that, and now, it seems, there was no way to undo this entry. She tries to distract herself with her music, sitting on the couch in her penthouse and pulling on the guitar strings, trying to come up with new material, trying to remember the old material. But she keeps on drawing blanks, and she cannot even remember her favorite songs, either her own or by other artists.

This frustration really gets to her, and she questions everything about herself. She questions even her own morality, and how much of herself she was willing to lose for this career that she dreamed about, hoped and prayed for, for the longest time. But she consoles herself, knowing that sleeping with Trenton really had nothing to do with career advancement. The contract was signed long before he made his way into her bed. And he did come at her from the premise of building a real relationship. Or did he? She doesn't know anymore. Trying to think back on everything that they did before they consummated their relationship frustrates her even more, though, and eventually, she just puts her guitar down.

She paces the length of her living room, not sure what to do with herself. She tries to remember if she has showered and then remembers that she showered, and then bathed, all in less than an hour. Clearly, she was just trying to wash the memories of Trenton off her. She cannot believe that someone who was so kind, so gentle, so absolutely tender with her, could turn into such a dick. She thinks of his dick, and against her will, warms between her thighs. She hates the fact that even now, even after everything that he did to her, she still wants him. How can she break this hold that she knows that he knows he has on her. His arrogance really is remarkable, but not entirely misplaced, she thinks to herself, thinking of Live Records' reputation as being one of the best labels in the country.

She pours herself a glass of wine, and then a glass of champagne, not sure which she will drink. 'Pull yourself together Toni,' she tells herself as if saying these words out loud to herself will automatically make it so. She knows that it won't though and that she will have to be a little more proactive about purging herself of Trenton. She doesn't want to, though. Why can she not shake him off her, the way she just shook off her robe. She walks naked onto the terrace now and stands against the breeze. The cold is strangely comforting.

Toni sips on the bubbles first, trying to come up with a plan to break herself free of this chain that Trenton has tied around her. She never considered herself promiscuous, but she thinks that it really isn't being promiscuous if she isn't in a relationship with Trenton. And he made this very clear. He slept with someone almost immediately after sleeping with her. Hell, he probably slept with many someones. She thinks of the hope that she had entertained, that she would be the woman who would change him, bring him out of his bad boy dark side. But that ship seems to have sailed.

She finishes her glass of champagne and then goes to get the glass of wine. She knows what she needs to do, to break this emotional deadlock that she finds herself in. But she also knows that she needs a little bit of Dutch courage to pull this off. She will go out, and she will find a handsome stranger to work out whatever longing, whatever yearning she still has for Trenton. After finishing the glass of wine, she goes inside, moisturizes herself, puts on perfume, and a sexy cocktail dress, and goes downstairs to meet the cab that she called as she locked up her penthouse.

Trenton is also thinking, hard, about Toni. Who the hell does she think she is? She cannot just come into his life and undo what he has known about himself for the longest time. She cannot just come into his world and think that she knows him, suddenly, thinking that she will somehow change him. He cannot think why he even entertains this situation, knowing that he can, and will, have whatever, and whoever he wants. Fuck Toni, he thinks. Fuck her.

There is a stalemate that seems to exist between them, and the worst thing is that they don't communicate this feeling with each other. How can they, though, when they are feeling the same thing for different reasons. It really feels like they are stuck out in the ocean on two islands, separated by an ocean. Toni knows that she doesn't want to feel the way she is feeling for Trenton, but she knows too that it is too late, and that she has fallen for him already. She will un-fall though, she tells herself. Trenton, on the other hand, hasn't accepted that he is in love with Toni. He knows that he likes to fuck her, but that is it. That just has to be it. It can't possibly be anything more.

Toni thinks about the sight in Trenton's bedroom and uses this as her fuel to get into the groove of what she really feels like she needs to do. She really needs to motivate herself, because try as she might, she had already started to think that they were in a relationship. Now that she knows that they are clearly not, though, still she finds the thought of another man touching her difficult. What Toni knows though is that she really needs to get passed this place in her head that is limiting her, holding her back from living, because Trenton clearly hasn't let anything hold him back. Hell, things have probably not held him back even when he was playing the wooing game. She takes a cab to the Latino part of town, somewhere where she can really lose herself, somewhere where nobody knows who she is, or who she is going to be.

Toni has always found Latino men attractive, and she wonders why she never explored this interest before. Why has her entire lovemaking been limited to black guys, and recently, one white guy? Tonight that is about to change, she tells herself, as she chooses a bar that looks just decent enough to be safe and she exits the cab. She walks into the bar and realizes immediately that this is just what she needs. The atmosphere is electrifying in a chilled sort of way, almost as though everyone in the space was just about to break out and dance, but after their current drink. It was filled with the promise of a good time.

She spots another promise in the

form of Eduardo, who is the first man to come up to her and introduce himself, offering her a drink. "Are you meeting up some friends or what?" he asks, wanting to know if he is in with a chance quickly. He is, his height, his build, the look on his face that says that he knows his way around a pussy, these all count in his favor. Toni must have said no, because a moment later, she is sitting with Eduardo in a corner, exchanging pleasantries that both of them hope will lead to something more, soon.

"Do you wanna get out of here?" he asks after three drinks.

"Sure..." she says, almost too eagerly. Maybe it's the alcohol, maybe it is just the fact that she really just wants to be naked with Eduardo now so that she can start to work through her issues. Whatever it is, they are soon headed towards Eduardo's truck, and soon enough, they are driving the couple of blocks to his place. Toni is nervous, but there is nothing about Eduardo that says, serial killer.

They arrive at his apartment, and the first thing that Toni notices is how tiny it is. It isn't unlike the apartment she moved out of before moving into her penthouse. She really has come a long way, and now she seems to have taken a trip back into the dark side. So what, she tells herself. Fucking around with Richie Rich really hasn't served her too well, and now she just needs to have her needs taken care of. And if she can satisfy Eduardo in the process that would be great too.

He offers her a drink, and she says no. She really just wants to get this on and get started, before she loses her nerve. And she really is starting to doubt whether or not she has the gumption to go through with this. Maybe she should give Trenton another opportunity to explain himself. There are way too many maybes running through her head, and so she pulls Eduardo towards her and kisses the taste of whiskey out of his mouth. He is a little surprised at first, and then soon gets the message, and kisses her back with an intensity that she can safely say she has never felt before.

They get naked too quickly, all Eduardo. He seems too skilled in the art of undressing a woman, and himself. He is obviously skilled at a lot of things. He has done this many times before, she thinks, and so she is comfortable with being with him. She isn't so comfortable when she sees his cock, though. It is thick and long, longer than any dick she has ever had the pleasure of being with. She knows suddenly that she has bitten off a little more than she is able to chew, but she will try.

Eduardo lifts her off the ground and carries her to his bed. It is hard and unmade, but she doesn't care, because no sooner has he placed her down on it, his lips find her pussy, and then his tongue. It reaches so deep inside her so quickly that she gasps, trying to sound like she does this all the time, but unable to. He really takes her by surprise, and she cannot hide this. She lets out a loud moan, and then a louder one. Then she screams as he digs deeper still into her cunt with just his tongue.

His tongue moves inside her with a beauty that she doesn't even know how to comprehend. She doesn't know when he even puts on the condom, or how it is that he managed to find one large enough to go over his massive tool. He gets her wet, so wet that when he removes his mouth and replaces it with his cock, it slips in easily. Only half of him will fit inside her, but half is all either of them need to make this night a beautiful one. As he starts to fuck her, and she is surprised by how easily he moves in and out of her.

She knows that he isn't all the way in her, and she wonders for the moment if he will be satisfied with this. But then she forgets about him, appreciating his cock but forgetting its needs, at least for the moment. There is a moment where they both forget, both of them lost in the moment completely, so that a little more of Eduardo slips into her pussy, lodging itself deeper inside her. She cannot take it, so that she holds his midsection off herself, trying to relieve herself of him a little.

This is not possible, though, and he digs a little deeper into her. She cannot breathe now so she cannot kiss him, barely making a sound. She knows that she will need to get air into her lungs soon, but how can she think of getting air into herself when she is worried about being speared with a scepter through her cunt. It is really a most uncomfortable invasion, and it threatens to become a little more uncomfortable as he digs still deeper into her. She closes her eyes and tries to imagine herself anywhere but here. This, too, is not possible.

Toni really needs to bring herself back in the game. She wanted a distraction from Trenton, and that is exactly what she got. Now she has to focus on making him feel good, and herself too. There must be a middle ground that they can reach, a place where both of them will really enjoy this interaction. But Eduardo really seems to be enjoying it more than Toni at the moment, and there are moments where Toni thinks that she might get him out of her. She holds on, though, knowing that she should start feeling good any moment now.

This moment could not come sooner. Her pussy is stretched so far to the back that it feels like the elastic holding it together might snap. But it doesn't, and soon it is feeling very damn good. She cannot believe it, that she is suddenly enjoying it, and it feels like, for the first time, she might have an orgasm. He fucks her gently now, so gently that it belies the size of his cock, and she has an orgasm to rival all orgasms. It worked. It really worked. The distraction that she sought is definitely present and accounted for. She hopes that suddenly Eduardo will actually fuck her harder.

He does. And she starts to sweat around her belly, as he brings her closer to having another orgasm. It seems though that he will cum first because he is fucking her harder and harder. When he does have an orgasm, she is having another one too, and this is beautiful. There is something unexpected about this because you don't expect simultaneous orgasms from one night stands. But here it was, and all its magnificent glory. They are both sweating profusely now.

Eduardo pulls the condom-covered cock from her slowly and then removed the condom. He sorts it out and then returns to where she is lying on the bed. She looks at him, wondering what is going to happen now, thinking that maybe it is over, and maybe this distraction is about to remove itself from her presence. She waits for him to ask her to leave or to offer her a ride to wherever. He doesn't though, putting the second condom over his still-hard cock, and mounting her again. He doesn't speak to her now, saying everything that he needs to with his cock.

They fuck all night, really fuck all night. Each round sees Eduardo go deeper and deeper into her pussy. She feels all stretched out when they have their final orgasm, and she has forgotten every man that she has ever been with. Eduardo was worth the trip to the dark side, and worth the hard bed that he fucked her on. He was worth a lot of things. When she finally gathers herself enough to shower the next day, he is still sleeping. She is glad, not wanting the awkwardness of the post-one-night-stand.

She calls a cab once she has let herself out of the apartment, needing to see where exactly she is, looking for street names. In the cab, she is finally safe, and finally alone so that she exhales hard. She thinks that she should at least have left her number next to Eduardo. But that is not how these things work, she knows this.

When she gets home she pours herself a drink that it is definitely too early to be having, but she takes it, to her bedroom, gets into a comfy shirt, and curls up in bed. She is glad that she has a TV in her bedroom, needing the distraction of the sounds, her eyes closed. She really needs to sleep.

12

In the studio, Trenton seems to know that Toni got up to mischief over the weekend, because he is seriously offish with her. She doesn't care, tries to ignore his renewed bad attitude, telling herself that he really has no right to be as concerned as he seems to be about what she gets up to outside of this studio. The studio really is also starting to feel like a prison, and she hates it. She tries to concentrate on the task at hand, but with the knowing stare that she is getting from Trenton, it is more than just a little difficult. Still, she tries to ignore it.

He is really involved in the process now, though, and not in a good way. He talks to CJ, loudly, about Toni, and she hears everything. Again she tries in vain to ignore what he is saying, but she is finding it more and more difficult to concentrate on what she is doing. She knows that she is really happy that she managed to get some action over the weekend, and is glad that it was with Eduardo. He has satisfied her so much that she knows that she doesn't need to be fucked for a while. So she can really focus on making music, but this new environment is more than a little uncomfortable.

"Do you have to be here?" she asks Trenton when they eventually take a break.

"I can be wherever the fuck I decide to be..." he answers, leaving her again to pick at her food, turning again to talk to CJ. He wants to know from CJ if Toni is going to be able to produce anything worth anything in time.

"It will be easier if you let me work, and waited to be called in to come and listen to what we've come up with..." she says in response to the question that was not asked of her in the first place.

"You will do what I say when I say it. If you don't like it, then you know how the door works..." he says, obviously trying to rile her up. She will not let him get to her. She knows that he is looking for any excuse to break the contract, but also, thanks to her attorney, someone that she has actually been able to pay for his services now, that he cannot do anything to her or her career for at least the next six months. She has time to produce a good album, and this is exactly what she intends to do.

"Is there a problem Trenton," she asks, needing him to articulate what is actually bothering him.

"The only problem is the one we will have if you don't deliver..." Trenton says, and he leaves the studio, at last. CJ is left wondering what the hell is going on here, and feeling an added pressure to make this upcoming album awesome.

Toni knows that Trenton is just playing up his power. He really has nothing else that defines him accept the fact that he owns Live Records and the fact that he can make or break an artist. He seems determined to break Toni, but she will not go down without a fight. She has fought long and hard for her life as it now is. And she will not let Trenton's childish behavior negatively affect her progress. Why the fuck did she sleep with him in the first place, she asks herself?

She works on the music that is almost melting together in her head now, appreciating the structure that CJ brings. There is something about Trenton's behavior that is really throwing her off her game, and she hates it. She wonders what her life will be if she has to go back to the way things were, but she tries not to think about it. All she has to do is get through the next few hours, then she will go home and regroup, thinking up a strategy for dealing with Trenton. She must find a way to manage him.

He makes it difficult, though. Because as soon as she gets home, there is an invitation to a party at Trenton's house. She knows somehow that she will not be able to get out of going, and so she immediately starts to think about what she is going to wear. The party is on Wednesday, and she knows that although she really doesn't want to be going out during the week, she must get used to these parties, and she may as well get used to them now. She does wonder, though, if Trenton was responsible for this invitation, or if it was one of his assistants just going through a list that they were given.

All of the next day she works hard in the studio, but she spends an awful lot of time discussing the party with CJ. She wants a date, wants someone who will be in her corner, and have her back if Trenton decides to attack her again. She thinks of asking CJ, but she isn't sure if he will not want to take one of the many women that she knows he has to be his date. She knows what these parties mean, and what happens to them, and so her apprehension is not entirely unfounded.

"You wanna go together?" she asks him eventually. "Not a date-date, but just to hang out together, and take pictures with the paparazzi. You can do what you like with whomever you like..." she continues, giving him permission for things that she really has no right to feel like she can control. But her nerves are really getting the better of her, and she is rambling. When CJ agrees, though, she can almost not hide her relief, churning out two beautiful ballads in in a single afternoon.

She doesn't go to the studio the Wednesday of the party. She feels the need to make an impression on Trenton, and on the other executives that she really hasn't seen for a while. She spends most of the morning at a spa, getting her face and nails taken care of, and having a series of massages. Then she makes her way to the trendy stores on Rodeo, and shops for an outfit. She buys several options, knowing that she is really glad for her new spending power. Nothing can take this new power away from her, and she will present herself as a real star tonight.

Toni is worried though about what the papers will make of her date. She thinks that even if they say that she is dating him, though, she doesn't care. She is just going to a party with her producer, at the owner of the label's house, and so she puts these thoughts back, way back in her head. She walks into her apartment, and looks through her purchases, trying to make the best possible decision. Toni knows that Trenton will be watching her, and he will be looking for her to put a foot wrong, waiting with keen anticipation for any reason to give her grief.

She decides to wear a short T-shirt dress, in black, with hints of gray and silver. Silver stilettos and a silver clutch complete her look. She wears long spaghetti string earrings, also in silver, and pulls her hair into a ponytail high on her head. She looks at herself in the mirror, thinking that maybe she should let CJ know what she is wearing. She thinks that this is a bit juvenile, though and that if they rocked up at the party dressed similar, this would fuel rumors that they planned this, and therefore they must be together a couple. She just hopes he isn't dressed too differently to her.

When he arrives to pick her up just after 8 PM, she is happy to see him in black jeans and a red shirt. This works for her, and they look put together, together, without trying. She is relieved. They stop over at a bar just before Malibu and have a drink. The party will only get steam from around 10, so they don't want to seem too eager, too excited to be there. CJ has been to many such events, and he knows how they work. Toni is only now getting used to these parties, and she is very careful not to come across this way, though.

They have more than one drink, though and eventually get to the party at around 10:30. This is perfect timing too because there are other people that are just pulling up to the front of the house, people who demand more attention from the paparazzi than just an upstart and her producer. They slip into the party relatively unnoticed, and CJ makes his way to the first champagne tray that he can find. He hands a glass to Toni, and they start to work the crowd.

Toni finds herself looking for Trenton, wanting to place him in this situation. She really needs to know where he is so that she can avoid him at all costs. He will hear that she was here, but there really is no need for him to be in her face. She doesn't want to be in his face either, thinking that there is something about her that has really pissed him off, although she doesn't know what. Shaking this concern from her, she loses herself in conversation with CJ and a couple of executives.

They discuss her progress and her

upcoming album. CJ is really impressed with her, and with the work that they have managed to do. When Cole joins them, he kisses Toni on the side of her face, happy that he is the one who actually spotted her. CJ is a brilliant producer, and if he says that she is doing well, then she must be. There is a lot to be said for her raw talent, and the way they are working it, she is really promising to be an exceptional star.

The conversation flows easily, but Toni feels that she is getting too attached to CJ like she is almost limiting his movements. She excuses herself, saying that she needs to go to the bathroom, just to give him space to breathe, and to talk to other people. Toni doesn't go to the bathroom, though, but instead, she gives herself a tour of Trenton's house. It isn't anything spectacular, by her standards. She doesn't like the excess of it or the art décor feel, but she has to admit to herself that at least it is nice.

She finds herself looking for Trenton again, but she cannot find him. She finds herself drawn to his bedroom, and tries to fight the urge to walk up the stairs, though. She remembers what happened the last time she was here, and the last time that she was in his bedroom. Unable to shake this image from her head now, she walks back outside. She really knows nobody here, besides CJ, and Trenton, but one of these men is in conversation with a beautiful girl, and the other is nowhere to be seen. She grabs another glass of champagne and makes her way to a group of men that look like they too don't really belong here.

Now she relaxes, in conversation with a drummer, a guitarist, and a few vocalists. All of them are also recent signings to Live, so they have this in common at least. They speak easily about the music industry, and with how their lives have changed, and are still going to change. They talk about their old lives and about the way they had lived before this opportunity presented itself. This conversation really seems like it would be better placed in a pub on the other side of town.

Trenton suddenly comes into view. He walks out onto the terrace with a woman on either arm. Toni is suddenly breathless, not sure why, but she cannot help what she is feeling. She looks around for an escape, tries to find CJ so that she can have someone to hold on to. She sees him too, but he is really making headway with the woman he is talking to it seems, and so she knows that disturbing him right now might not be the nicest thing to do. She smiles and nods at the guitarist still speaking to her, and to the group, but she can really hear nothing that is coming out of his mouth.

He is walking towards them now, and she wishes the earth would swallow her up. Never before had she known this feeling, but now, she really wishes that the ground would open up. She looks at her feet, hoping that he will pass them, and move on to people who are more interesting than her and the group she is standing with. No chance, though, and before she knows what is happening, he is standing in front of her, kissing the woman on his right arm. He knows that this has everything to do with her and that he is trying to unnerve her.

It is working too, because she is suddenly very dry, wanting another drink. Thankfully a tray passes by her, and she reaches for a flute. She drinks half the contents of it before she says hello, hating the tameness in her voice. Why does this man who has shown her that he wants nothing more to do with her get to her so much? She really cannot stand feeling like a small child who has to be put in the naughty corner, to think about what she has done.

She hasn't done anything though that she can think of to warrant this treatment. She puts it off to something in him, some deep seated need to control everything and everyone, and the fact that she has been mostly uncontrollable. Fuck him, she tells herself, not sure if she is saying this out loud. He has a conversation with the other musicians around her before turning his attention to her. As he speaks to her, he moves his lips from one woman to the other, so that she knows that this is definitely for her benefit. He really wants to get to her.

She listens to what he is saying but hears nothing. All his words seem to blur into one long sentence, and she cannot make head nor tails of what he is actually saying. Toni really wants to get away from him, away from this situation, and away from this party. There is no chance of this now, not until CJ decides that he wants to leave. She must be strong, and pull herself together. Taking deep breaths now, she gathers herself as best she can. Trenton sends his tongue onto the one woman's neck, and she turns away from this exhibition. She really doesn't need to see this.

Trenton is determined, though, determined to make her feel smaller than she already feels, and it really works. Toni looks at the men surrounding her, and she wants to pull one of them to her and kiss him, just to show Trenton that two can really play this game. But she thinks better of it, and she also regrets not taking Eduardo's number or leaving her number with him. She obviously hasn't worked Trenton out of her system completely. At least she knows that she has the option of getting some action in LA because she is not unattractive, and also because she knows that she is more than willing to put out.

She thinks though that Trenton is really turning her into a version of herself that she doesn't really like. She isn't the kind of girl to go out in search of random one night stands. And that is what she seems to be doing, in retaliation for Trenton's bad behavior. Surely there is another way to do this, another, better way for her to handle these onslaughts. And they are relentless, Trenton now sticking his tongue down both women's throats, and moving his hand up and down their thighs. Toni really just needs to remove herself from this situation.

When Trenton asks her to join them in the bedroom later, this is the last straw for her. She turns away from the group. She laughs, though, letting him know that this might be an option, just because she thinks that this is the right thing to do, and she walks away. She goes to the side of the terrace that looks down on the beach, and she strains her eyes to see the waves lapping up against the sides of the beach. The tide has come in, and so she knows that walking down on the beach might not be the best thing right now. She just sips the remaining champagne from her flute, wishing that she was a little drunker than she is right now.

A hand is suddenly on her shoulder. She wants to turn around and see who it is, but if it isn't Trenton, then she really doesn't want to see who this person is wanting her attention. She turns eventually and sees the guitarist standing there in front of her. He asks her to play a tune with her, and she says that she hasn't brought her guitar. He says that he has his instrument here so that they can just jam. And nobody would object to this free concert. She asks him what he wants to sing, and when she hears him whisper the title of a well-known ballad, one that she knows, she agrees. This is another way for her to distract herself from what Trenton is doing she thinks, so she gets ready for this impromptu performance.

There is no stage now, not tonight because there was no performance planned. But the guitarist is eager, as are some other performers present. Toni had no plan to perform, but now she is making her way up to the top of the terrace stairs that come directly out of the house and positions herself in full view of everyone on the terrace, including Trenton. Trenton looks at her, wondering for a moment what is going on, knowing exactly what is happening when the guitarist, named Eli, joins her, armed with this instrument.

When he starts strumming, and she starts singing, the whole space goes eerily silent. It is obvious that here stands a star, and her star quality is really second to none. She makes the song her own, truly her own, and most of the people in the space don't even recognize the original song in the notes that belt out of Toni's mouth. When she hits the high note, there is a visible chill in the space now, and everyone, absolutely everyone, including Trenton, is completely and utterly mesmerized. She knows that she is good, she knows that she is really good. But it is these moments that confirm for her just how good she actually is.

She takes in the applause, really takes it all in. She sings a few other songs, and then takes the guitar from Eli, strumming out a few chords, letting a few harmonies escape her. Then when she is done, she hands the guitar back to her partner in crime and then makes her way down to where CJ is still clapping his hands together. He pulls her to him, and holds her tightly, too tightly. Then he hands her a glass of champagne that he took off a passing tray, and they bring their glasses together. CJ smiles at her and then pulls the woman he was talking with earlier to him, introducing her to Toni. The two women greet each other, talk for a minute, and then Toni excuses herself.

Toni finds herself looking for Trenton again. She cannot find him, and she starts to panic. This is not just a mild anxiety either too, but a really panic. She looks hard for him, and when she doesn't see him at all, she doesn't want to be here anymore. What is this game that she is playing with herself, she wonders? Why is there such a thin line between her wanting to be with Trenton, and wanting nothing to do with him? She calls a cab and then makes her way inside, to wait out of sight for the car that is on its way to pick her up, and which will be there in about 45 minutes.

As she walks through the terrace doors, she spots Trenton at last. She sees him going upstairs with the two women that have been hanging on him for the entire evening. He is obviously about to take things up a level, and thank them with his body for sticking with him throughout the evening. Toni fights the urge to follow them, but loses this battle, because as soon as they disappear off the landing, she is walking up the stairs too, following them from a distance. When she gets off the landing she sees them disappearing into his bedroom, she follows them still. She thinks that they might close the door, but they don't, strangely enough. Toni looks around for anybody who might see her, and then when she sees nobody, she goes up to the door and peeps inside, curious to see what might happen now.

It feels like she is witnessing a car accident. She really wants to look away, but she can't. She wants to see when these cars collide, and how many casualties the incident will leave in its wake. There is half a wall that obstructs her vision of what is happening inside the room, though, and she knows that if she wants to see everything, that she will have to go inside the room. She does, not sure why still not sure what it is that has her wanting to see Trenton with these other women. What she does know though is that she really wants to see what is about to happen in the room, and when she is inside, she too doesn't close the door. She just stands beside the wall that leads to the main bedroom space and watches them interacting with each other.

Her stomach turns as she watches them kissing. It is intense, like the kissing you would see in a porn video, and she wonders if this is the way Trenton likes it. He was very gentle with her, and she wonders now if this was for her benefit, or his. The notes she is making in her head bother her, though, and she thinks that perhaps she should leave. As she turns to walk out of the room, though, Trenton's pants suddenly come off, and she cannot peel her eyes away from him. She knows that there is not a chance that she will walk away from this scene now, so she hides a little more behind the wall, and watches the scene play out in front of her, like a film playing out in silence in an old-time movie theater.

13

Both women go down on Trenton's cock with their mouths. They lick his dick all the way from the balls to the head, each sticking to the side of the massive shaft. Toni watches with interest, to see how the suck him, and what parts of it he enjoys. He doesn't give anything away, though, as the women work harder and harder on his cock, trying to draw some sort of reaction from him. Trenton just looks down at them, watching them work on their parts of his cock, ignoring his nuts completely. Then suddenly one woman takes his balls into her mouth, the other sucking his cock completely now, and Trenton lets out a little moan.

The women work with precision on his cock that makes anybody watching think that they had done this before, with him. They seem to know his cock, its proportions, and also its responses to what is about to be done to it. Toni finds this intriguing, and she wonders why she has not yet done this to Trenton. She wonders why he hadn't initiated it, and thinks a million thoughts that make no sense when said out loud. She says nothing out loud, though, remembering where she is.

She really shouldn't be here. She looks to the door again, almost open, slightly ajar, and she thinks that maybe she should slip out of it. But she is so mesmerized by what she is seeing in front of her that moving is really not an option for her right now. Seriously conflicted, she pushes herself closer up to the wall, and takes a deep silent breath. She remembers the last time she was in Trenton's bedroom, the look on his face, bordering on disgust. Could it be that she was just a very well-kept secret, on that he was only comfortable being naked with away from here?

Thoughts creep up on her again, and she tries to shake herself free of these. She opens her eyes willingly now, really wanting to see what is about to play out in front of her. The women stand up, and she watches as Trenton's fingers find their pussies, going into them, all the way in. The women moan so loudly, tossing their heads this way and that, so that Toni thinks that they will see her, but noticing that their eyes are closed. They really seem to enjoy this fingering, and as it continues, Toni notices that Trenton's cock is a pulsating raging beast now.

He obviously wants to be inside them. She thinks that if he had two penises, he would penetrate them simultaneously. Toni almost laughs at this limitation, thinking that for all Trenton's money and power, this is the one thing that he cannot change about himself. Trenton keeps on fingering these women, with just one finger, and then two, working with such skill on them that you can see that he has had lots of practice. The experience that he has is so obvious now, so clear that he looks like he could finger them expertly in his sleep.

Hands move up and down his shaft, four tiny hands, and the look of it is magnificent. Toni is transported in her mind to the harems of old, where one man had the pleasure of many women, and where men were virile enough to handle these many pussies. She watches with renewed eagerness, wanting to see when, and how, Trenton is going to penetrate them. She wants to see which of the women he is going to enter first, although, they are both so similar that it really doesn't matter.

She watches as he slips his fingers from one, and then the other, and then watches as he fucks their hands for a little while longer. She watches as he goes to the drawer and pulls out a strip of condoms, putting one on in one seamless movement. It really is impressive to watch, and Toni remembers when she was last with him, how effortlessly he put that particular condom on. He is really an expert at all things sexual, it seems. Toni is suddenly very aroused. This happens much against her will, though.

But when the mounting begins, she is more than a little taken aback. She watches as Trenton enters the one woman quickly, too quickly, and this catches even the woman by surprise. She takes it in her stride, though, and as soon as he begins to thrust, she gets comfortable rather quickly. Toni watches as the second woman comes from behind Trenton, between his legs, and apparently takes his balls in her mouth. She too seems to be more than a little comfortable with this position and taking her fingers to herself. She also wants to be fucked, but she is willing to wait her turn.

Trenton fucks the hole that he is in for the longest time, though, and the woman on his balls gets bored a little. She moves off his balls, and then sends her tongue against his asshole, which catches him by such surprise that he almost pulls out completely from his perch. The woman eating his asshole though is a little relentless, though, and he is pushed into the cunt that he is fucking. Her hands are on his ass, pushing him down and parting them so that she has better access to his hole.

She really licks it now.

Knowing that he isn't going to get away from this, he lets her eat out his ass. He focuses instead on the hole his cock is occupying, and he brings this woman to a beautiful orgasm. He keeps on fucking her, while the woman on his ass has her fill. As soon as she lifts off him, though, he pulls out of the pussy he is just fucked dry and turns onto his back. The condom is so full of semen that it trickles out the side of it as he rolls it off. Then the woman who hasn't been fucked goes down on his cock and sucks it clean. As soon as he is cleaned up sufficiently, she now rolls another condom down his thick, long shaft.

She mounts him, and she starts to grind against his cock. The other woman takes the breasts of the woman jockey in her mouth, and she sucks on them as the rider brings herself to orgasm. Trenton stays hard long enough to manage this too, and when he starts to go limp, he watches them as they remove the condom and work together to lick him clean. They are really eager beavers, and as they suck and lick his cock, he is suddenly hard again.

Toni has seen enough now, though, and she turns to walk out of the room. As she does, though, the light in the room catches her movement and casts a long giveaway shadow across the floor. The room is suddenly filled with her shadow it seems, and she stops dead in her tracks. She cannot believe that they are going to see her, but there is no way for her to get out of the room without being seen by them if they look her way.

She moves back behind the wall and holds her position. She doesn't move for the longest time, not knowing that Trenton has seen her already. He smiles to himself, knowing that the thigh that is just visible around the corner belongs to nobody else. If a show is what she wants, then that is exactly what he is going to give her. He pulls one of the women towards him, and as he turns himself onto his knees, he pulls the woman onto her knees. He pulls her towards the edge of the bed, and then he teases her asshole with his uncovered cock.

He drops some spit onto his throbbing head and proceeds to pierce forward with his cock, using every muscle in his ass to drive his cock into the tiny hole. The hole gives easily, and he slaps her butt cheeks as he begins to thrust. He fucks her hard, so hard that she lets out scream after scream. He proceeds to fuck her harder still, and she is panting. She hides her head in the sheets and lets him fuck her, continuing to pant into the sheets which are curled up around her face now.

Trenton is careful not to look at where he knows Toni is standing, though, so as not to startle her. He closes his eyes instead and drives his cock repeatedly into the woman whose asshole he is now obliterating. He really is going to town on her now, and the woman seems to be enjoying it too. The other one positions herself the same way that the one being fucked is positioned, willing Trenton to please take her too, to please give her asshole the same treatment that her friend is getting. He obliges, of course, and after pulling his cock out fast, he almost immediately inserts it, rock hard and ready, into the second waiting asshole.

This woman is more used to being

fucked in the ass it seems because she doesn't let out a single sound. The harder Trenton fucks her, the more she smiles, and the more she seems to glow. There really seems to be a halo around them now, the way this woman, and Trenton too now is glowing. He fucks her furiously, really needing to cum now. Just before he does, he pulls his cock from her ass and sprays his load on her back. To Toni's surprise, the other woman is again sucking on his cock, cleaning it like a real expert.

When Trenton gets up and goes to the bathroom, he pisses very loudly, and Toni cannot bring herself away from this sound. This turns her on, to her surprise, and she is suddenly warm between her thighs. She really wants to get out of here now, though, and as soon as the sound of Trenton doing his business stops, she slips out of the bedroom, not caring if the other women in the room have seen her or not. She doesn't care about them at all.

She walks down the hall and passes the steps. She finds an empty bedroom, and she goes inside it. She closes the door and locks it. Toni sits on the bed, and she pulls a pillow to her, screams into it several times, and then tosses it on the floor. Why does Trenton get to her like this she wonders? He has obviously made it clear that he is in no way interested in her, and that he, in fact, wants nothing more to do with her. She makes up her mind to get some action, right here, right in Trenton's house. How dare he think that he can get away with treating her like this?

She gathers herself and makes her way out of the room. As she exits it, though, she sees Trenton exit his own bedroom, the women in tow. She is sure that they couldn't have showered yet, and this sort of disgusts her. So what, though, she tells herself, that is really not her problem. She watches them leave, watches them go down the stairs. Then she follows, thinking which one of the men who have shown her attention tonight she will make very happy.

Toni works the room on a real mission now. She talks to all the men in the various spaces of the house, and she flirts with every single one. But as soon as they suggest that they go somewhere a little more private, she has an excuse. She tries to shake this from herself, not sure still why she is holding on to thoughts of Trenton. She knows just that she is, and that disrespecting him by hooking up with a guy in her house is not her style. Far from it, in fact.

She must get away from here, and she must do so in a way that will get to Trenton as much as he has got to her. Eventually, she settles on one of the Live executives, a perfect specimen of a man. He is obviously much older than she is, older than Trenton even. Toni knows from the research that she has done on Live that this man, Harrison Jones, is more of a silent partner. She will never see him again after this, not unless she runs into him at a party here, or at the offices of Live. She knows too that he is really just interested in a one night stand, something that she has convinced herself that she needs to right now.

Harrison is really a showoff, which serves Toni really well all things considered. He needs to find Trenton with Toni in tow so that he can let him know that he is, in fact, leaving with her. Toni is relaxed, thanks to the number of glasses of champagne that she has had since she witnessed the porn video upstairs. She just smiles as Trenton and Harrison have a bit of a face off, but are rather cordial with one another as the older man lets him know that he is going to hit the road.

Toni and Harrison get to his car and Toni starts to have second thoughts. But it is too late now, and she is certainly not a tease. She will give Harrison the night of his life, and hopefully, he won't be a half bad shag. She starts to wonder, as they drive away from Trenton's mansion if she is going to suggest that they go back to her place. It is too late for them to make up their minds about whose place it is going to be because Harrison is driving in the direction of his house already.

He is very touchy too, and his hand has spent more than the requisite time on her thighs by the time they pull into his long driveway. His house is impressive, more so than Trenton's, and Toni makes a mental note to use this place as a reference for her first purchase when she is ready to enter

THE BILLIONAIRE'S SONG: THE COMPLETE SERIES

the homeowners market. It is really a beautifully constructed building, and she is more than a little mesmerized. She is so impressed that when they make it through the front door, she cannot resist asking for a tour. Harrison obliges her, never tiring of showing off his house.

By the time they are done with the tour, Harrison is quite hard now. He manages to control himself enough to get a bottle of champagne from the kitchen, though, and in his bedroom, he pours them both a glass. They drink it rather quickly, both of them wanting to get to the main event quickly, for different reasons. Harrison finds Toni very attractive, and so he wants to see her naked. Toni, on the other hand, wants to know if this will be worth her while.

When Harrison goes for Toni's clothes, she is relieved. She helps him out of his too, and when they are both naked, both of them are very pleased, although they don't say it. Harrison is very excited now, wanting to get inside her quickly. But he wants to taste her too, and so he puts her on his bed, hands her another drink, and while she sips on the bubbles, he goes down on her and makes the most delicious meal of her pussy. When she has an orgasm, he feels the need to mention that he has had a vasectomy, and she knows that this means that he doesn't want to use a condom.

She thinks about it for a minute and then decides to throw caution to the wind. She just smiles at him, letting him know that it is okay for him to go for it. Toni hasn't had a look at his dick, though, and she thinks that she will not get a chance to see it before he is inside her. He moves her up higher on the bed, and then he goes on his knees in front of her, giving her the first clear view of his cock at last. She is happy, more than a little happy because his dick isn't very long, but it is thick, and it is neatly circumcised. She knows that she will at least be satisfied if he lasts long enough to bring her to another orgasm.

Harrison mounts her at last, and she feels really filled. It is a beautiful feeling, and she certainly loves every moment of it. He thrusts into her with so much power that she feels that she is being pummeled by his cock.

Harrison also is enjoying it, really enjoying it too, and while he is fucking her with incredible power, he is also fucking her with the most incredible patience. An hour goes by, and he is still fucking her, bringing her to orgasm after beautiful orgasm. Not once does he give her the indication that he is going to cum, or even that he needs to.

When she has had what feels like her millionth orgasm, he pulls out of her and goes to pour them a drink. She is confused, this breaking all the protocols of a one nighter, but she is certainly not complaining. Then he is inside her again, and she is loving it, all over again. She feels like he is really fucking her for the first time, his energy not waning once, and his erection going nowhere but deep inside her. Toni feels like she is going to lose her mind. And she also feels like she is going to lose her cunt now, at the rate that Harrison is going.

She realizes at last, what it is. He must have popped a few little blue pills to help him along. She certainly has no regrets. And when he eventually does cum, he explodes a massive load inside her, and she thinks that she can feel it seeping out of her. Harrison is really exhausted, and he turns over and falls asleep almost immediately. Toni really needs a shower now, though, and so she goes to find the bathroom. She gets under it and lets the water run over her body, and then moves the lather around on her, cleaning herself from the events that currently unfolded and have left her really very exhausted. She needs to get home, though.

After she finishes, drying herself and getting dressed, and hoping that Harrison didn't set his alarm, she calls a cab, reading his address off the mail pile in the kitchen. She manages to let herself out of the house and waits in the street for the taxi. When the taxi arrives, she is relieved, although she knows that it was probably rude of her to just leave without saying anything. There is nothing to say, though, except thank you, and she believes that she has thanked him enough with her body. She gives the driver her address, and as he makes his way to the other side of town, she is more comfortable as they get closer to what is familiar to her.

A few blocks from her apartment building is a pub, though, and she suddenly has the urge to stop and have a drink. She pays the taxi driver and goes into the pub. Seated in a corner, she orders a drink and then pulls her phone from her purse. She checks it, seeing that she has a lot of missed calls and messages from CJ. Shit, she completely forgot about CJ. She checks the time and thinks that it is too late for her to call him. She sends him a message, letting him know that she is safe, and thanking him for going with her to the party. CJ responds almost immediately. Clearly, he is also a night owl. A few minutes later he is seated across from her at the 24-hour pub.

They talk and laugh about their respective conquests for the night. CJ really is like the bigger brother that Toni never had, and she finds it easy to talk to him. She can really tell him anything, and so she finds, after a few more drinks, that she is talking about Trenton. CJ doesn't mind, though, and he really listens to what she is saying. Watching her talk is really beautiful. CJ is already getting hard just watching her. He knows though that he has crossed the line into the friend zone, so this is totally off the cards for him right now.

The next few days are easier than the past few weeks have been, especially for Toni. This is because Trenton has stayed away from the studio for the most part. He must really have given up on her now, and she finds that with every day that passes, she finds it easier to just not see him. Not seeing him is the only thing though that makes her not want to fuck him. She really still wants him inside her, and she wants to call him by a title she hasn't bestowed on anyone in a while. She wants to call him her boyfriend. But this seems to be the last thing on Trenton's mind because he is avoiding her it seems. Or maybe he isn't avoiding her at all, and he has just gone back to his old, charming self.

After they wrap up the studio work on this particular day, Toni really just wants to get home. She wants to get dressed and go out on the town, in the Hollywood part, and really blend in. There is something new about this life that she really is starting to find appealing. She decides that it is now time for her to really immerse herself into it and that she is going to have fun with her new role in life, her new station. She is going to be a recorded artist very soon, and she is going to have a single out very soon. This will catapult her into the world of the recording artist, and she needs to be as prepared for this as she possibly can be.

On her way home, she stops for dinner, though, needing to eat, but also needing to see what the vibe about town was tonight so that she knew what to wear for her expedition. She watches people moving in and out of The Ivy, one of the trendiest eateries around, and she checks to see what everybody is wearing, and more importantly, how they are wearing it. She wishes that she had asked CJ to join her, but she knows that she needs to be a big girl now and that with her big girl panties on, she will become a fully-fledged Hollywood hit. She has no doubt about her impending success, but there are still reservations, deep in that place where caution reigns supreme.

She decides to walk home from the Ivy and loses her bearings a few times. The sun has really said goodbye to the day so that she starts to think that maybe it would be safer for her to just jump into a cab and get home already. The air is crisp and inviting, though, so she really just decides to take advantage of it, and walk anyway. She keeps on walking through the streets of LA, and she really enjoys the feel of the city now. She really just loves being here.

Finally, things start to look familiar, and she knows exactly where she is. She crosses a few streets and then goes around a few more corners, getting closer to her building so that she slows down her pace, and settles into the now night. She finally gets to her block, and she turns into her street. Toni really is starting to feel like she belongs in her life like she is at last taking ownership of her existence. She walks blindly down the road, not looking at the details of her street anymore, having seen them enough for them to really just become background to her now, even at night. The city takes on a whole other life at night, and she really likes it. It makes her feel alive. She spots something that doesn't quite fit on her street, though, as her building comes into view. She needs to take a minute to catch her breath.

14

Toni doesn't know what to do about the man sitting on the steps leading up to her building entrance again. She is really tired of Trenton and his games. As she walks up to him, she thinks that maybe she should just let him in again, and hear what else he has to say to her. There is one thing on her mind, though, and it has been on her mind for a while now. She wants him to sleep with her again, not sure if it is because she wants to hook him with her punani, or if she wants to just use him the way he used her. But using him seems like an absurd idea, and as he follows her into the building, she makes up her mind to just sleep with him, if he wants to.

She knows that she wants to.

He has really gone on roller-coaster tangents, making her feel like she is really just another piece of ass, just another one of his conquests. She tries to forget this, though, at least for the moment, knowing that two can certainly play that game. He has been a total dick over the last few weeks, making things more than a little difficult for her. Yes, she knows that he has the keys to the kingdom, that he holds her career in his hands. But she knows too that he cannot just renege on their contract, hopefully. For now, she tries to forget all the things he has said to her over the last while and the way he has treated her. She decides that she wants him and that she will just ignore the nagging feeling, tugging at her pride, for the moment. She is proud, but not at the expense of her pussy. She knows what she wants.

They walk into her apartment, and he says nothing still. She ignores him completely and goes to the fridge. She gets them both a drink, pineapple juice, just so that she doesn't give him the wrong impression. Still, Trenton says nothing, and Toni is at peace with this silence. She drops her shawl on the sofa and then opens the doors that lead to the terrace. The sun is already setting, and she wonders why he is here, and what he wants to say to her now. Has he not insulted her enough? Has he not even apologized, not once, for any of his behavior over the last weeks. Especially the last time she was at his house. She really doesn't care, though, she can't. Toni knows what she wants from him now, and she has really decided to play the game.

"So, here we are..." Trenton says, finally. This statement makes absolutely no sense to Toni, but she really doesn't care, not focused on his words.

"And where exactly is that?" Toni asks him after finishing her pineapple juice.

"Here, alone..." Trenton responds.

"Yes, and?" Toni asks, wanting him to get to the damn point.

"And nothing..." Trenton says, finishing his juice too now. He walks over to where Toni is standing on the threshold to the terrace and places his hands on her hips. She knows immediately what he wants. Is this his way of apologizing, she wonders? If she gives in to him, then he will assume that all has been forgiven and that they can move on from here. She isn't ready to forgive him, though. She is ready to fuck him. But forgiveness is something that he will have to work a little harder for.

She isn't sure if she should move out of his grip, or if she should turn and kiss him. Kissing him would definitely send the wrong signal to him, though, so she fights the urge. She closes her eyes and feels his fingers moving up and down over her hips. Electricity moves through her and settles quickly on her pussy, and she knows that there is nothing that she can do to turn back from this now. Toni just stands there and lets him move his hands over her hips and onto her thighs now.

He comes up close to her now, rubbing his cock against her ass now, really wanting to undress her now. He isn't sure though how she will respond to this, knowing that he has really treated her badly over the last while. He is really throbbing, though, really wanting to be naked with her.

Conflicted, though, he isn't clear in his own head why. This is too much for him to process now, though, now that he has a raging erection that wants some attention. He needs to know if she is going to give him what he wants, though, and he needs to know now. Otherwise, he is really just wasting his time.

Trenton lifts her skirt, high, and takes the elastic holding her panties up between his fingers. He starts to pull it down slowly, very slowly, waiting for her to object, expecting it in fact. Then he pulls it down a little faster when it is clear that she isn't going to protest. She really wants this too, more than he does it seems. But none of them are saying anything to each other now, so this isn't clear. What is clear, when Trenton gets her panties off completely, is that she is going to let him take her.

There are many things that he wants to do. He wants to go on his knees and taste her pussy on his lips. But he doesn't, not wanting to waste any time in case she changes her mind. He pulls on the strap holding her skirt up, and it falls to the floor. He wants to take her top off, but again thinks he is in a race against time. He needs to get his own pants off, quickly, and when he pulls his jeans down to his knees, he thinks that this is the only distance from his ass that he is going to get his trousers.

He doesn't know why he feels the need to rush it. He doesn't want to, really he doesn't. Trenton has a deep respect for Toni, and he has feelings for her that he doesn't want to admit to himself. Now, though, now that he is treating her like a whore, he thinks that he will finally work through these perceived feelings and get them out of his system. He pulls her to the sofa and pushes her over the edge of it, so that her upper body is on the seat of the chair, her ass and pussy hanging over the edge of it, waiting for him. He wonders how wet she is.

Using a single finger, he feels her pussy. He uses his middle finger, which is his longest, and he works it up her cunt. It is warm, and it is exceptionally wet. He feels like he has just won the lottery, and he pulls this finger out of her slowly. He smells the finger, and this hardens his cock even more. He wishes that he can just take his jeans off completely, but he doesn't, knowing that he needs to at least get his cock inside her and start fucking her before the truth of what is happening settles on her, and she comes to her senses. How could she, he thinks, let him make love to her after the way he has treated her? There is no way, and so he knows that this really is a bonus, a reward for something that he did not do. He doesn't deserve this.

He digs into his pockets while finding her cunt again with his middle finger. He fingers her slowly, as he undoes the condom, removing it from its wrapper. Then he removes his finger from her pussy and puts the condom on. He comes up close behind her and finds the entrance to her with his cock tip, and then slides himself into her. She lets out the softest moan, and he knows that he is home. Slowly, very slowly he starts to thrust into her, and then pull himself out. Half out, and all the way in, half out, then all the way in again. She continues to moan softly, and he knows that she is enjoying it. He relaxes now, knowing that she will never stop him now. She couldn't stop him even if she wanted to now.

She starts to moan louder, and he knows that he is bringing her close to climax. But he doesn't fuck her any harder or faster than he has been. He just keeps sending himself into her over and over again and consistently filling her with his cock. The sounds coming from her are beautiful, and he closes his eyes, enjoying these sounds like a symphony. There are fewer things that bring him as much pleasure or have brought him as much pleasure in the last while, as bringing pleasure to Toni.

With other women, he has never felt the need to be overly concerned for their pleasure. They have been satisfied purely as a byproduct of his own satisfaction. But Toni is different. He knew this from the moment he saw her. And he has battled with feelings for her for the longest while. Even now he is struggling, trying to make her less than what he knows she is to him. She seems to know this, though, and she seems to be happy with something that she isn't even saying. He knows she is not stupid, and she is not desperate. She must just really like him.

He regrets his behavior over the last while a little more. But then again his bad boy streak surfaces, the black wolf inside him winning against the white one. He pulls her hips up towards him, and he goes deeper into her. He fucks her hard now, thinking that if he can cum before her, and then leave her hanging, that this will be funny, and this will mean that he doesn't really care for her. He does, though, and try as he might, he cannot bring himself to orgasm before she has had at least one.

Trenton doesn't beat Toni to orgasm, and when she cums, she hides her face in the seat of the sofa. She is almost embarrassed that she has let him take her, but knows that it would be less than hospitable if she were to evict him from her pussy now before he cums at least once. The last thing she wants to be is a bad hostess, and so she lets him continue his assault on her cunt. It seems to be taking forever, though, and she isn't sure if it is because he is enjoying it, or if it is just because he had sex with a couple of women before coming to her and is therefore in no hurry to cum now.

Either way, it is too late for her to think about these things now. He is already inside her, and he has yet to cum. She has had another orgasm, though, and this sort of sets her mind at ease. She knows that as long as he keeps thrusting into her that she is assured of orgasms. At least that is a consolation. She is really enjoying it, though, and the fact that he isn't saying anything to her allows her, for brief moments, to imagine that it was somebody else. The feeling of his cock inside her though is so signature, so Trenton, that she cannot use her imagination to get away from him for any stretch of time. He keeps at it so that she is no longer sure if he is doing it for her pleasure, or if he is just unable to cum. His cock is still rock hard, though after she is brought swiftly to a third orgasm, so she knows that he still wants to be inside her.

Her third orgasm is loud, and she cannot hide her pleasure even if she wanted to. Knowing that her pussy must be tired, he pulls himself from it, slowly. He looks down at his cock, throbbing, aching for a hole. He wonders if she will let him into her asshole, knowing that there is of course only one way to find out. He needs to test first, though, to see if she will be able to take him, or if in fact, she has taken cock in the ass before. He correctly assumes that she hasn't.

He parts her ass cheeks, exposing the most perfect little asshole. It is so obviously tight that the need for him to test it with his finger is really unnecessary. He really wants to, though, not even remembering the first time he had a virgin ass. Actually, if he is honest with himself, this is an experience he has not had, ever. Many women have pretended to be virgins in this priceless hole, but after a few strokes, they were riding his dick with what can only be described as lots of experience.

Trenton thinks to drop spit on the hole but then thinks better of it. He has another plan. He takes his tongue onto the tiny tight hole and licks once. She tries to move away from him because this is an experience she has never had before. She doesn't know what to make of it, and so she tries to wriggle away from him. He holds her firmly in place and sends his tongue onto her asshole again, this time lingering there, moving it around, occasionally teasing it, as though he were going to enter her asshole with his thick, wet tongue.

Over and over, he tries for entry, but as soon as he makes some headway, her asshole contracts so much that it threatens to take his tongue completely off. He is determined, though, almost relentless, and he tries again to fuck her asshole with just his tongue. Eventually, it starts to give, and he is digging his tongue deep into her asshole quickly. He is really digging into her now, holding her firmly in place, and making sure that she is not going anywhere. She isn't sure how she feels about this, but soon enough it starts to feel very good, and she relaxes into it.

He knows that he needs to get his cock into her, and his dick is really throbbing now. It is actually aching in the condom now, and he wishes that he could just take it off to free his cock and enter her bareback. But he knows his reputation, and he knows that she might not be comfortable with this, so he holds himself back. But it really takes everything in him. His respect for her though is uppermost in his mind, and he knows that he must just control himself.

Eventually, he cannot take it anymore. He comes up to standing and positions his cock near her asshole. He tries to hold back from thrusting into her, and he just teases her with the tip of his cock. Again her asshole contracts, tighter than even it did before. He tries again, just the tip, nudging the head into her asshole, which is really very tight now, making entry impossible. He is really determined, though, almost as though he knows that he will only cum if he gets inside her asshole. The hole finally stops resisting, and his head slips inside it.

He cannot pull out the tip, not once it is inside her. He can also not go any further into her, knowing that this must be very uncomfortable for her. Trenton starts to rub her back, towards the bottom of it, and then onto her ass cheeks, rubbing hard, really digging his fingertips into the soft flesh that he finds there. Then he starts to enter her slowly, distracting her with his fingertips on her back. This works too because even though it really hurts like hell, the fingers up and down her back are so beautiful that this pain is more than a little bearable.

Then he is half way inside her, and he stops moving altogether. He knows from the sounds that she is making that she is more than just a little uncomfortable now. He starts to pull out his dick from her slowly, and he listens for the telltale signs that she is enjoying it. These sounds don't come, though, and he sends his cock into her again, just halfway. When he pulls out again, she starts to pant, and he knows that this is just her way of making the adjustments necessary for her to take him. This goes on for the longest time, and he really starts to think that he should just pull it out of her completely because she is just in too much pain.

Suddenly the panting becomes the softest moaning, though, and he knows that he is at last making progress. Still, though, he fucks her ass really slowly, not wanting to rush this. Each stroke is delicious, though, and she is also starting, at last, to enjoy it. She never thought that she would, but now that she is, she doesn't know why she had never let another man fuck her in the ass before. Toni is glad though that Trenton was one of her firsts, though.

He goes deeper into her now, knowing that this added length will be uncomfortable, but also knowing that she will adjust soon enough. When he gets into her with a third of his cock, he knows that there is no more of him that will fit inside her, not today, not given the fact that this is her first anal experience. He settles into the fact that he is only going to get her to take about two-thirds of his cock, and so he relaxes into this, fucking her with just this much dick.

The urgency to cum is suddenly lost. He is really just enjoying that she has let him into her sacred space. He has incredible control over his thrusts too, and he knows that it is probably just because it is Toni. He keeps on rubbing her back, and then her ass cheeks, and continues to send his dick into her. It is truly the most magnificent ass that he has fucked in a long time, maybe even ever. The beauty of this experience has him close his eyes now, especially now that he is sure that she has finally relaxed into this absolute invasion.

He starts to work himself towards his own orgasm now, and pretty soon there is no turning back. He knows that he is going to cum soon, and provided he doesn't go any deeper into her, she will let him. He thrusts a little more eagerly into her now, but no deeper. Closer and closer to blowing, his eyes open, and he looks at his cock moving in and out of her asshole now. The sun has set, but he has a clear view of the action on her ass because of all the lights coming into the space from all angles. It is quite something to behold.

Soon enough he is cumming, and he cannot hold himself back. He pulls her closer into his cock, lifting her off the couch somewhat now so that she has her hands on the seat of the sofa now. She knows that he has cum too, and she is relieved, happy too that she brought him to an end in her asshole, something she has not done with anyone, ever. When he pulls out of her ass, the hole is shut again, and he goes to the bathroom to sort out himself and the condom.

When he comes out, she is completely naked now, her clothes on the floor. She holds two drinks, champagne this time, and she holds one out to Trenton, not sure if he will take it. He does, though, much to her relief. She excuses herself and goes to the bathroom to shower, finishing her glass of bubbles before getting under the spray. She isn't sure if she wants him to come in after her, but when she starts to shower, she forgets about Trenton completely, thinking only about the first experience she just had. It was interesting, to say the least.

She comes out of the shower with a towel around her, and her glass in her hand. She doesn't even look for Trenton, knowing that he is gone, probably left to battle whatever demons fucking her invokes in him. She really doesn't have time for this, really not caring what he thinks of her, or himself anymore. She cannot do this to herself. There are more constructive things that can occupy her mind, and her body, she thinks. Trenton is just a very capable lover, though, and she cannot help but feel that there really is more to him than meets the eye.

Trenton is home within the hour. He thinks of what just happened with Toni, and what it has done to him. He doesn't hate the way he feels anymore, just doesn't. He accepts it, completely, for what it is. After pouring himself a drink, a too-stiff vodka, he too is naked now. He thinks of showering, but not. There is just too much on his mind, and he needs to figure out what is happening for them right now, what it means for the two of them. He knows, at last, what he wants it to mean.

He admits to himself, at last, that he is in absolute love with Toni, and that this has thrown him off balance. She has taken everything that he believed about himself and turned it on its head, and she has done so without even trying. She wondered how she had let him get under her skin. He wonders exactly the same thing, remembering the first time he saw her, the feeling that sprung up inside him, the way he made him feel. Not a believer in love at first sight, or any other such bullshit, he fought it, really fought it, until he couldn't fight it anymore. He knows now that he is addicted to her, and drawn to her, like a moth to a fucking flame.

Trenton regrets leaving her apartment now, leaving without saying goodbye, without saying anything. Why has he behaved so badly, for what? What has he gotten out of the way he has treated Toni? And why is she still giving him the time of day? The answers to these questions are uncomfortable for him again, and so he doesn't try too hard to articulate them. He goes into the shower instead and washes his past off him. He really scrubs off the bad behavior that he has exhibited over the last while and makes a silent promise to himself to change his ways. He has to change, or else risk losing Toni forever. The thought of losing her is even more uncomfortable for him than the acceptance of his love for her. He must just stop fighting it. All he has to do is stop resisting this tide that seems to be flowing with or without his permission.

He takes up his phone now and starts to work through all the numbers on it, all the women that were on standby for him, whenever he had an itch that needed scratching. He takes a deep breath and then starts to delete the numbers. He feels a little relief, a little freer, and he likes it. Trenton has another drink and finished his phone purge. As soon as he has completed the entire purge, he takes a step out onto the balcony and thinks about how and where he will see Toni again. He decides to give it a few weeks, and if he doesn't feel any need to go out and get another woman in his bed, then he will call Toni, and invite her over.

15

Trenton looks like he is genuinely ashamed. Toni has no response for this look. Twice bitten is a game that she really isn't prepared to play with him. She hates that she still has a nagging feeling inside her, though, a feeling that she really hasn't felt before. She knows somehow that he needs her, more so even than he wants her. This is a new experience for him too, she thinks, and she has got to decide whether or not she will actually walk this path with him.

How can she, though, when he has played hot and cold with her so often. How can she take his hand and guide him down this unfamiliar path when she herself doesn't know the way? She really has no idea how to get him over to the light, or even if she wants to. She thinks that maybe she is to blame for his behavior, making him question himself and what he thinks he knows about himself. Is it possible that this is as much her fault as it is his?

He comes up to her and puts his hands on her hips. She hates that she responds immediately to his touch. She almost comes into him now as he lands his lips on her neck. He mouths 'I'm sorry, ' and she hears it so loud as though he were screaming it. Toni has no response for this either, knowing just that she really wants him to be touching her. And now, she is here, in his bedroom, where he has bedded many women obviously, and she feels, for the moment at least, like she is just another face in the crowd. Is she prepared to be another notch on his belt?

Why is she questioning it, though, she wonders? If this is the game that he wants to play with her, then surely she is as skilled as he is at this game? She knows that she isn't though and that she really wants more from him than she thinks he is prepared to give her for the moment. People change, though, some more slowly than others, she reasons, and as he finds her lips with his, she knows that she is prepared to work with him to bring about the changes in him that she so desperately desires.

She kisses him back, all resistance falling away now. She lets him undress her too, and as she stands naked in his bedroom, she has a million thoughts racing through her head. The most present thought though is of what is about to happen here, and she wants to make it good this time. She remembers all of the times that they made love before, remembering that she never was very assertive, thinking that it is time for her to bring out her own little bag of tricks. She thinks to herself, thinking that maybe it is just a sexual relationship, but knowing instinctively that it isn't. She knows that she is committing to something real and that Trenton is also trying to commit. She gives him a mental ten points for effort.

Toni kisses Trenton for a while longer, and then she takes off his t-shirt. Then she works on his jeans and slides them down his long legs. He steps out of them, and as he kicks them away, she is working on his underwear too. He lifts his legs out of his underwear too and is standing naked too in his bedroom now. The lights are on, and so the contours of all his body and hers are visible. She really sees him, for the first time, and him her, and this experience seems suddenly very new. She goes on her knees completely now, so that she is comfortable, and she breathes in his cock. The smell is familiar to her, so familiar that she thinks she knows what it is. Cinnamon, she thinks, but she is just not sure. She smells his balls too, really breathing in the smell of him, and enjoying it.

Trenton looks down at her, surprised by this new turn in her behavior. He likes it, but he isn't sure if she is just doing it to please him. She never seemed forthcoming sexually before, and he thought that she was inexperienced. But she is obviously not because she is sliding his cock into her mouth now, and going almost all the way. He watches this, and he is completely and utterly impressed. Trenton doesn't move at all, just letting her work with his cock now, letting her mouth dance on his dick so that she becomes more comfortable with his length. He knows that his cock is long, more than just a little, and so she needs to adjust to it in her mouth. Everything in him wants to thrust into her mouth, but he realizes that he respects her too much to do such.

He watches her work on his dick. It feels incredible, almost as though he is having his cock sucked for the first time, ever. She is also very good at what she is doing, moving her mouth over his cock with suck skill, with just enough teeth, and just enough tongue. It is really a beautiful experience, and he cannot take his eyes off her. Then she is licking his head, and she makes a meal of his dick-head, driving him more insane. He cannot take this pleasure anymore, and he pulls his cock out of her mouth. This is because he thinks that he is going to cum, and he doesn't want to insult her by spraying his load into her mouth. Although he knows that she probably won't mind, but still, he controls himself, pulling himself away from her, leaving her a little surprised.

She doesn't want to continue sucking him now, still confused with what just happened. Then Trenton is suddenly rubbing his dick against her lips so that she knows that it is okay for her to keep sucking on him. She does, and again he is lost in the euphoria of the situation. He really wants to please her too, but she seems to be enjoying sucking on him too much. He is enjoying being sucked too so that he just keeps sliding his cock in and out of her mouth. Her teeth, tongue and most of her mouth attack his penis again, and at last, he closes his eyes.

He wants to ask her to suck on his balls, but again, out of respect, he doesn't. He just watches her move on his mouth, hoping that she will eventually suck on his balls. He actually starts praying that she does, and when she is sniffing his balls again, he thinks that it is going to happen now, at last. When she does eventually send her tongue onto his nut sack, he almost jumps out of his skin. There is something about his balls being sucked that really drives him insane.

When she nibbles on his sack, she notices that he is really in it now. There is something that she can do to please him, she realizes, and so she bites a little harder. Then she sucks on his balls again, taking one orb at a time into her mouth and then sending her teeth into the skin again. He holds her head in place now, and she really bites into his balls now, making him feel even nicer. Trenton runs his balls over her mouth, in her mouth, and then against her lips. She takes them in her stride, really enjoying the taste of him now.

After a moment, he is sliding his cock into her mouth again. He cannot believe again that he is actually sending his cock into her mouth, loving it more and more, the more relaxed he gets. Again he feels like he is going to cum, so he pulls his cock from her mouth again, and sends his balls into her mouth, after rubbing them against her lips for a little while. She remembers how he responded to her teeth earlier, and so she bites into his nuts again. Trenton moans loudly now, unable to hold himself back, not able to control himself.

When she goes for his head again, he tries his best to hold her back, and pull her from his cock. He needs to please her for a little while, at least. He lets her suck on him a little while, and then just as he is about to cum, he pulls it from her mouth and pulls himself together enough to pull her to her feet. He looks down at her now and smiles. He will make her feel good now, very good. He knows this, and so he lifts her off the ground and moves her to the bed.

He lays her down on the edge of the bed and parts her legs. He kisses her inner thigh and then moves to the other one. Then he kisses the top of her thighs, and then all the way down to her knees. He kisses her up her thighs again and then finds her inner thigh with his mouth again. Then he sends his teeth into the soft yet firm flesh between her legs, and she pulls herself towards herself, trying to gather herself quickly, just so that she doesn't come across as too eager.

Then he kisses her pussy, on the outside of it, and she feels sheer bliss. As she is processing this bliss, he suddenly sends his tongue into her, and she is in another state of euphoria. He fucks her so tenderly with his tongue that she feels like she is going to have an orgasm almost immediately. She doesn't though because just as she feels like she is going to climax, he is sending his tongue deeper into her, and resetting her clock. The whole world seems to be coming to an end now, a most beautiful and wonderful end. This is getting more and more intense for her.

When he is fucking her with his whole tongue now, she cannot breathe. She feels like the moment is now a long, languid orgasm, but it isn't. There is a moment that she thinks that she cannot breathe, or think, but she is screaming loudly, very loudly, so that she feels like she cannot take it anymore. Then he stops moving his tongue, and she wraps her legs around his head, encouraging him to continue fucking her with his tongue. He does, following her cues, and making her feel like she is going to climax again. There is a way for her to get him to keep fucking her, but she feels like she has done enough, encouraged him enough. His tongue moves around her deep inside now, and she just relaxes, her breasts heaving high and low, panting through her mouth.

Trenton holds her down on her belly, and really sinks his tongue into her deeper. She cannot move anymore, cannot think anymore, and then she feels that she is going to cum now, really blow. She starts to cum, and she cannot even hold herself back from having a massive orgasm now. She blows a massive load, and really spray into his mouth now. Trenton is shocked, but he likes it. He appreciates that she has had an orgasm, and appreciates that she has really enjoyed the beginning of their lovemaking. She takes a moment to recover, but she cannot. She shudders, really shudders, and she cannot control herself even if she tried now. There is a moment where she eventually catches her breath, but catching her breath doesn't help her at all because she just continues shaking. She shakes for the longest time, and then, at last, she gathers herself sort of.

Trenton takes his teeth now and places them on her clit. He nibbles on it and then bites a little bit harder. She takes herself on a trip in her mind and tries to distract herself from this situation, not wanting to cum so soon after her previous orgasm. There is nothing that she can do about it, though, and Toni is soon having another orgasm. She sprays another load into his mouth, and she looks down at where his head is moving between her legs aggressively now. Then he licks her cunt clean and drops a few tender kisses on it.

He smiles to himself, happy that he brought her to two orgasms in such quick succession. He starts to kiss her up and down her belly and then finds her belly-button with his lips and tongue. He really enjoys the taste of her, licking around her naval, and then licking up and down her sides. The sweat falls off her like little rivers, and he laps it up. Trenton really enjoys the feeling of her too, there is a slight shiver, an almost quiver, and he holds her down with his lips.

Toni closes her eyes, and she arches her back so high that her head falls back. This is going to be absolutely beautiful, as beautiful as it has been already, and so the top of her head is touching the sheets. Her forehead too makes contact with the sheets, just to give an indication of how high her back is arched, and how far back her head is tilted. She starts to grind her waist, pushing her cunt up against his arm, and then against his chest, trying again to find his mouth. But then he finds her tits with his mouth, and she is thrilled, forgetting the need between her legs for the moment.

He licks her nipples with the tip of his tongue and then uses the whole surface of his tongue to lock up the sweat on the surface of her breasts. She puts her fingers in his hair and pushes him down harder onto her black mounds. He sucks harder, and then a little harder still. She really loves it, grinding her midsection against his, really needing to find his dick now. Still, it eludes her, though, and the frustration starts to build deep inside her.

She really wants him inside her now, but then his lips land on her neck and she forgets temporarily about her need. She is so distracted by his lips moving over her body that she almost forgets where she is, focused entirely on what she is doing. It is really just so very nice. There is nothing else that comes into her head now, no stray thoughts. All her attention is on the man that is about to mount her now, and this is where it needs to be. She knows this, very, very, well.

When Trenton is on her lips, he seems to be a little distracted, but his lips don't leave hers once. She realizes that he is fumbling with his penis, probably putting a condom on. Where it came from, she doesn't know, but she is just glad that he has one on hand. There is a moment of hesitation, and then both his hands are free to move all over her body again, and his whole mouth is on hers now. She sends her tongue into his mouth repeatedly, and he takes it in, loving the taste of it. They share a hell of a lot of saliva, swallowing it over and over again.

They really taste each other, literally eating each other now, loving every minute of it. Toni isn't even aware that Trenton is already working his way inside her. She is just so wet, so ready for him, that the initial impact of the penetration is easily accepted. But when he is all the way inside her she needs a moment to breathe and so she pulls her mouth away from his. Trenton also is not aware of how deep he went into her, and this catches him by surprise too, so that he stops moving altogether.

When he returns his mouth to hers, he starts to thrust gently into her. She loves every movement, and then some. He is enjoying it too, because for the first time he is really present in the moment, enjoying every part of the woman that he is making love to. They are both present in the moment and feel like they really are one. Moving in and out of each other, and through each other, and then in and out again, they make love until the morning, without even realizing it.

By the time they finally fall into each other, completely exhausted, Trenton just holds Toni in his arms, grateful that she is here. He appreciates without saying it, how much she is investing in him, and the fact that she is really trusting him with herself. He looks at her, himself still totally immersed in her, and he smiles, thinking about his life, and how, if he is willing to do the work, it will change forever, just because she is in it. He slips himself out of her at last and lets her catch her breath. She falls asleep.

Toni dreams of what this could mean for her. If it goes wrong, then her career could really be over. She has never considered herself a weepy singer, so she will not be able to draw from the experience of his rejection of her if that is how it goes. She knows from recent experience that when he does reject her, work is strained and difficult. But she really is trusting herself to him, and hoping beyond hope that this doesn't go south. She wakes up a few times, and when she sees he is still here, and that they are still in his bedroom, she goes right back to sleep.

She wakes up to a tray of fruit. Trenton has brought it into the room, still naked, and semi-hard. She wants to eat, but she also thinks of brushing her teeth. There is just something about this ritual that she deems necessary. She asks Trenton for a toothbrush, and he smiles at her, offering her his. She thinks he is joking, but when they are both standing naked in the bathroom, she is handed his toothbrush. Toni thinks about this for a minute, and then she puts some toothpaste on it and starts brushing her teeth. There are some people that might think this is weird, but not for them. They are very comfortable with each other now, and everything about being together suddenly seems easy.

Trenton comes up behind her and watches her in the mirror as she works the toothbrush around in her mouth. She really is a sexy woman, and she doesn't seem to have a morning face. She doesn't even have morning breathe, but Trenton knows that women are fussy with things like this. He watches her a moment longer, and then he goes onto his knees, parting her legs. She isn't sure what is happening, but she knows that there is nothing that she can do to stop it from happening. Toni thinks of the fact that she hasn't showered yet, but she doesn't care too much. She thinks that if he did not like the taste of her, then he wouldn't be sniffing between her legs, sending his tongue into her snatch.

She rinses her mouth while he works on the entrance to her punani. She drops his toothbrush into the sink and holds on to the side of it, steadying herself. Toni raises her ass a little, parts her legs a little more, giving him more access to the parts of her he so desperately seeks. He takes full advantage of this, holding her hips, and pulling her harder into his mouth. He sucks on her for a while, and then sends his tongue into her again, fucking her with all of it. She feels like she is happier than she ever has been. Actually, she knows she is. And it isn't even just the sex, which is very nice. It is the fact that she now has a man that isn't perfect, but whose imperfections she really feels like she can work with.

Perfection is overrated, she has always thought. There is something about situations and people that are too perfect that has always bothered her. Trenton is so far from this, so far from anything actually, that she really thinks that she can mold him into her version of imperfect perfection. She is also not perfect, far from it, and she knows it. She accepts her imperfections and feels the need again to save Trenton from himself. But there is more to it than just that. She isn't even sure what it is, but she knows that she is willing to find out. There is something intriguing about the uncertainty of love, especially in the beginning. Yes, she dares to think of this as the beginning of love. But whatever happens, she intends to enjoy this situation, for everything that it is worth.

Trenton suddenly stands up behind her and goes into her cunt from the back. She knows that he isn't wearing a condom, but so what, she tells herself. There are ways to nip that it the bud soon enough. He works his cock up in her all the way and then starts to thrust immediately. The sounds coming from her let him know that he is doing a very good job. He is, and he keeps on thrusting into her steadily, making sure that she is comfortable, and then bringing her closer and closer to orgasm. The pending orgasm is pregnant with promises. And it delivers too because she blows so hard that she sprays on her thighs and down his front too, over his cock, which is still hard, still thrusting into her. She is in absolute bliss.

He remembers the feeling of her ass now, and his cock is suddenly harder. He brings her to another orgasm, and then he slowly pulls his cock from her pussy. Using her own lubrication, he eases his cock between her ass cheeks, and into her asshole. It goes in easily, but slowly. He knows that the last time they were together was her first time taking it up the ass, so he is very careful about his penetration. Once he gets into her, though, he really starts to thrust hard, loving the feeling of her, and losing himself almost completely now. He sends his hands around the front of her, and as he inserts his cock deeper into her ass, he finds her clit with his fingers. He moves his fingers in circles on this engorged flesh now, and fucks her gently, beautifully, and with an intensity that lets, you know that he has yet to empty out his morning glory.

Trenton brings himself to a wonderful end, slow and steady really winning the race, and then just as he starts to cum, he brings her to her third. He pulls himself from her very slowly and turns her so that she is facing him now. She holds him hard, pulling him into herself, and kissing him as hard. Toni knows that this is going to be a challenge for her, and for him too. But one thing is clear, and that is that they are both willing to put in the work required for them to make their relationship work. She decides not to think about this for the moment, though, and she loses herself in his mouth again. Trenton too is fighting with the thoughts of what is actually happening here. He is happy with where they are and optimistic with where they are going. They take their bodies, and their minds, back to the bedroom...